Anita Tyler and the Puzzles of Mass Destruction

Alex Mitchell

Published by Alex Mitchell, 2024.

ANITA TYLER AND THE PUZZLES OF MASS DESTRUCTION

First edition. March 11, 2024.

ISBN: 979-8891980273

Written by Alex Mitchell.

Also by Alex Mitchell

I dedicate this book to Denise "**Ghette**" Klein, the strong-willed supporter of my endeavors that are hardest for most to see at their original launch.

Chapter 1

Flashing lights and buzzes and beeps made Fatima Patel restless. Conversations buzzed about her in various tones, voices, and languages, making her fearful. At eighteen months, Fatima was not sure what about this made her squirm, but she held close to her two greatest treasures. One was her mother, and the other was Dolla, Fatima's dark-skinned Ragged Annie doll. Fatima's mother, Cora, rocked her as they tried to make themselves as comfortable as possible in the Clearmont Airport. But comfort has its limitations in an airport terminal. There was an automated disembodied voice that would give a warning about being aware of suspicious persons and unattended packages. The warning made everyone and everything in the airport seem suspicious; this and the fiberglass seats were bolted to a steel frame and welded to an iron post set in concrete.

Colton followed his mother. Colton's mother had let him wheel his suitcase. Colton was five years old and proud of his big-boy accomplishments. Colton's mother strolled, trying to find a seat in the terminal where she could be seated with her son. Valarie, Colton's mom, chatted nervously into her cell phone, assuring her husband that she would soon be boarding flight 1317 and returning home. There, Valarie thought near the mother and daughter.

"Look Bitch I don't give a shit who promised you what. I don't mean a God Damn thing until I sign on the bottom line." A portly man in a rumpled suit was having a private conversation with a cell phone and doing it in the most public way possible. Valarie and Cora looked over at the man, hoping he would take the non-spoken cue to lower his voice or, at the very least, choose the words he was using around children more carefully. "Ethics if horseshit. I can't buy lap dances with ethics. I need cold hard cash, and the other firm is offering two million more." The man on the cell phone continued his conversation. He winked at Valarie and Cora, indicating he did not understand how rude he was being.

"Attention all passengers for Flight 1317. The aircraft has arrived. We are in the process of cleaning and crew change. We plan to begin boarding at 1:15. We are on schedule and know you have your choice of airlines. We appreciate your choosing us." A snippy, robotic female voice sounded through the air.

Cora shifted to adjust Fatima, and Fatima dropped Dolla. Cora did not notice that Dolla had fallen, but Fatima did. Dolla's button eyes stared back at Fatima as she lay on the floor between the railing that secured the chairs.

"Colton, don't wander off. We will be boarding soon." Valaire called out as a command to her son. Colton did not comply. He pulled away from his mother and crawled between the stationary seating. Colton rescues Dolla and then hands her back to Fatima. Fatima accepted Dolla and smiled.

Right on schedule, the Airbus 319A would take off from the Clearmont Airport. One hundred and three passengers and eight crew members would be on board this flight headed for Portland, Oregon. On board flight 1317, there was a varied mix of people. The passengers represented all age groups, sexes, and nationalities. The one thing all one hundred and three passengers and the crew had in common was that very soon, they would all be dead.

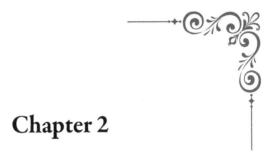

Chapter 2

The cruising speed of an Airbus A319 is five hundred fifteen miles per hour with a max speed of five hundred forty-one miles per hour. Flight 1317 flew toward its intended destination in the most routine of fashion. In the United States, an average of between three hundred forty-nine and three hundred seventy-six people die as a result of commercial air travel. In an average year in the U.S., there are approximately 45,000 flights.

In 2021, 2.2 billion people flew, meaning around 500,00 people per day. This makes flying one of the safest means of transportation.

"Well, Kid, I guess you are looking forward to a few days off." The pilot started, turning to the co-piolet in their secure environment known as the cockpit.

"Yeah, two days in a hotel in Portland, Oregon, be still my heart." The co-pilot responded just before seeing what looked like an infrared light beam. The co-piolet turned to the piolet and saw the pilot staring back at him. Seeing one another was the last thing man's conscious mind would record.

Two CFM56-5B 68.3-inch fan engines propel the Airbus A319. There is one fan engine on each wing. The right-wing exploded. The weight of the remaining engine, combined with the force of the explosion, sent the craft flipping end over end in a sideways summersault. There was the sound of lost and lost human lives crying out for salvation that created a cry that would scare the dead. Then, a second massive explosion sent shock waves in all directions. The second explosion was followed by silence. The following silence was not the peaceful silence of a spring morning but the silence created by a vacuum in human existence. Even birds seem to be holding their breath, trying to figure out the what and the how. Those of Flight 1317 now congregated in death.

Chapter 3

Harvey Newman walked slowly across the Oregon field, trying not to crush evidence beneath his all-weather boots. Harvey was a big man. Not fat but strong like a construction worker. Harvey Newman was the supervisor for his unit of The National Transportation Safety Board. Harvey was nearing retirement age but could not bring himself to make such plans. He was supposed to be off work, but Jerome had called him frantically, trying to get him to come to the site. The crash site was massive. No matter how large, It was too huge for a plane to have just hit the ground. An alarm bell started going off in Harvey's head. This is so wrong, he thought. Harvey removed the opera glass from his pocket and surveyed the area. Small teams of workers were flagging and tagging evidence all over the valley. Harvey spotted a mass almost three miles away that looked like a second crash site, but how could it.

"Good to see you, chief," Jerome confessed, meeting his boss. "Sorry to take you away from the day off."

"You probably saved me from going to jail for murder."

Jerome smiled. Jerome was a lanky black assistant supervisor with a degree in engineering—Jerome had a broad smile and an easy-going demeanor. Jerome and Harvey had a working relationship that they both enjoyed. "Who were you going to kill?"

"My daughter's new boyfriend. The young puck struts around all day with a woody wearing tight jeans."

Jerome knew it was his cue to take some of the pressure off his boss by letting him vent. "Katie is a good girl. You raise her right."

"It aint Katie that has me pissed off. When I was his age, I had a woody for everything in hot pants."

Jerome noticed Harvey staring at the second crash site, but Jerome was unsure how to bring it up.

"Okay, Jerome, let me have it. What the fuck is that up that hill, don't tell me a corporate jet decided to play chicken with a commercial jet and lost big time."

"Well, boss, that would make too much sense. That pile of burning rubble is the right engine from the commercial jet in front of us."

"So, the engine wasn't attached to the plane when it hit the ground?"

"That's my assessment," Jerome answered in his perfect English.

The men continued to walk the primary crash site. Harvey began bellowing orders to all the crew. Jerome scribbles feverishly on a notepad.

"So, what about the new boyfriend has you spooked?" Jerome finally asked.

"It is a fact that it isn't Katie that he is looking at when he gets these major erections. It's Donna, my wife."

Jerome tried to hide his laughter but could not.

"Yeah, laugh at my pain."

"Didn't you have crushes on older women when you were his age?"

"Shit, that aint the point. Donna is loving this attention a little too much."

"I see your point, and by the way, do you want me to call the F.B.I. or Homeland?"

"Both. I will be damn if we get caught holding the bag." Harvey looked around at the massive death scene. "Barbara Stanwyck."

"What?" Jerome asked.

"When I was a teen, no teenage girl could come close to matching up to Barbara Stanwyck."

"I am going to have to look that one up."

"And by the way, if you ever tell anyone I told you that I had a major hard-on for any woman other than my wife, I will have to kill you, too." Harvey, drying, joked and started walking up the hill to the second area of impact.

Chapter 4

Anita Tyler dropped her duffel bag at her feet and snapped to attention. Anita had been led to the office of Senior F.B.I. Agent Waldren Clarkson. Sargent Morehouse, a tall, muscular woman with a stern face, had been ordered to bring Anita Tyler to the F.B.I. Oregon office. Clarkson sat behind his desk, eyeing Anita but not saying a word, existing comfortably in the discomfort others felt in the silence of the room. Waldren Clarkson was a smart-looking middle-aged man with an official gleam in his eyes.

"You are dismissed, Sargent." Clarkson finally stated.

Anita still stood at attention, reviewing her past indiscretions in her mind. Anita mentally sorted through her recent sins, trying to think which landed her here in the F.B.I. office. Anita was nearing the end of her time in the army and looking forward to returning home to Lamont, Mississippi. One of her brothers was getting married in a small Missouri town, and it was a family tradition that no matter when or where one of the Tylers got married at the first opportunity, they would have a separate service for family and friends in the church where they were members.

"Turn around, Tyler; let me get a good look at you." Clarkson requested. Clarkson's office was small and cluttered with books, files, and folders. There were autographed pictures of past presidents on the walls shaking Clarkson's hand.

"Sir, may I remind you that sexual misconduct on any level is inappropriate?" The Sargent stated in a commanding tone.

"Sargent, what I find inappropriate is the fact that you are still standing in my office after I have dismissed you. So, to clear that up, if you don't leave immediately, I am going to call some of my teammates to drag you out as unceremoniously as they possibly can. You see, here in the Nation Security Branch, we deal with national security matters." Clarkson stared at Sargent Morehouse with a look that would melt stone.

Anita had two great passions; one was football. Her brothers had taught her to play quarterback. Anita played in the church leagues, and anytime she could put together a game. In the army, it had been easy to find women trying to stay in shape, and many did not mind playing touch football, even if they were not as good as Anita. Anita found that with a team of female soldiers willing to play, she could challenge women's groups from other divisions and branches of the service.

Anita's second passion was poker. She played poker well because she had learned to read the tells of her competition. This is why Anita did not fear Sargent Morehouse being asked to leave the room. Anita knew Morehouse had no idea why Anita had been called to this office and was useless in finding out why she had been asked to come here. Anita knew, however, that Morehouse did not want Anita to know that she had been left in the dark and wanted to stay just to find out what was transpiring. At last, a high stakes game, Anita thought, let's play.

Sargent Morehouse left the room in the military version of a snit.

"You were doing a pirouette." Clarkson reminded Anita.

Anita took a slow, full turn. Like Texas Holdem, it was her chance to pick up clues on her next move. Anita noticed the spine of a book that had been shoved beneath a pile of papers. Her father, S. Rowen Tyler, had written the book. Anita's father was a retired police chief turned writer. S. Rowen Tyler had been known to ghostwrite biographies for law enforcement officers, to use fictionalized accounts of stories from police and F.B.I. investigations, and to assist law enforcement officials at times. Anita could smell the pale smell of tobacco. Anita detected not a cigar smell but the lingering smell of smoke. The residual smell adheres to one's clothes after going outside for a smoke and returning. There was a space where some pictures had been removed recently, and nothing was replacing them.

"Eric, you and Carolyn get in here. You made a mistake." Clarkson opened the door and screamed into the hall as though his supplicants were waiting for his next word.

In an instant, a small, thin man in his early twenties appeared, followed by a woman about the same age.

"Who is this, and why is she standing like that?" The young woman was a large-breasted blond with overly teased hair and a tart perfume that smelled something a teenage girl might be wearing.

Eric and Carolyn started circling Anita, eyeing her up and down. This was getting to be a regular part of the routine, Anita thought.

"This, my dear children, is Anita Tyler," Clarkson answered.

"Nice body, but she can't be." Carolyn declared.

Great, Anita thought, two men in the room, and it's a chick that starts talking the nice body shit. Anita did have a well-developed body. She was nearing the end of her term with the military but had always taken her exercise seriously. Secretly, Anita dreamed of taking the field against a male-led team and quarterbacking her way to victory.

"Why is she standing like that?" Carolyn squeaked.

"She is at attention. No one has told her to go to at ease or as you were." Eric answered.

"How do we get her to stop? She is making my back and feet hurt." Carolyn assessed.

"As usual, you children have missed my point." Clarkson began. "There is no way she fits into the business suit you showed me. She will look like a cocktail waitress on her first training day."

"Are you the lawyer?" Carolyn finally addressed Anita, who stood at attention wearing an army tee shirt and camo pants.

Even people who are not good at reading people can frequently pick up subconscious messages from your tone or voice inflection. So, to this point, Anita had chosen not to speak. But the circle of lunacy was closing, and she knew it best to offer some insight. "No, that would be my sister Noreen; she is smaller than I am."

"You have a nice body, but don't look like a bodybuilder." Eric tried to clear up clumsily.

"Thank you. You're cute too, but that would be my sister Jody." Anita could see a slight glimmer of disdain in Carolyn's face at her retort. In a millisecond, Anita knew Carolyn had a beyond-professional interest in Eric. The quickness with which she tried to erase the scowl told Anita it was, to some degree, unrequited.

"So, shouldn't you be at UCLA training for the Olympics?" Carolyn asked in a proud-of-selves tone.

"Still wrong, girl. That is Sandra Max Tyler."

"Boss, I think you got the right girl but pointed to the wrong one in the photo you showed us." Eric tried to clear up the mistake.

"That is ridiculous because I don't make mistakes as your boss. Now, how do we fix it."

"Well, do you have a business suit in your duffle bag?" Eric asked Anita.

"If she does, it better come with an ironing board; the meeting is in less than a half hour," Carolyn commented.

"Sit," Clarkson commanded of Anita.

Anita flashed a look at Clarkson.

"That is where you put your ass in the chair, Tyler." Clarkson clarified.

Anita sat thinking it was not the command that sounded out of place, but the tone reminded her of her father. The book that was covered, she thought; this man knew her father, and the missing picture was of this man, Senior Agent Clarkson, and her father. But he chose not to lead with this information.

"You read." Clarkson slapped a thick folder in Antia's hands. "You or this folder do not leave this room under penalty of treason until I say so. Are we clear?"

"Yes, Sir," Anita responded.

"Carolyn, I don't care who you have to strip, but find her appropriate attire for the meeting. Eric gets her gear and the forms." The young duel shot out of the room without a single response to perform their assigned tasks.

Clarkson was about to comment to Anita when his cell phone rang in his pocket. "Yes, she is here now. No, she does not look like the great man at all. She is quite lovely." Anita could hear Clarkson whisper to the person on the phone. Another tell Anita thought; the great man was a nickname friends and family used for her father.

"Here she wants to talk to you," Clarkson announced, shoving the cell phone to Anita.

"Who is it?"

"My wife."

"Don't know your wife."

"And she doesn't know you."

Reluctantly, Anita accepted the phone. The woman on the other end of the phone sounded weak and ill. The woman drifted a little while talking.

"No, I don't see him smoking, but it does smell like he had at least one today," Anita commented on the device. "Well, I think he is wearing the second ugliest tie I have ever seen. My uncle Elmo has some uglier than that, but him being a rodeo clown and all, I sort of make an allowance..." Anita could finish the comment. Clarkson snatched the phone and was off. Anita was not sure what she was expected to find in the folder, but the instant she opened it, she was compelled by its content. It was an airline crash that wasn't a crash at all. Flipping through the security photos, Anita stopped on a picture of a small black child retrieving a doll for an East Indian child. Trust glowed in the eyes of the child, and confidence in accepting the trust ran in the little boy's smile.

"Sign these papers." Anita had been so engrossed in reading the file that she had not noticed that Eric had returned carrying a large box. Anita signed the forms to return to her reading, and Eric handed her a leather identification case. Anita opened the case, and there was a badge and a picture of her. The ID read Anita Tyler F.B.I.

"Whoa, hold on little due; what is this."

"Here is your issued weapon, a Glock 19. The boss says we all carry them in the field, and he insists that you carry a backup." Eric continued with his assigned duties of transforming Anita into an agent.

"This is the best I can do." Carolyn began speaking before entering the room.

"The blouse and skirt are nice but don't match," Anita observed, still reeling from what seemed like an overly elaborate prank.

"Yeah, suck to be you. But you need to change before the boss returns and says we didn't do our jobs." Carolyn assisted Eric in turning his back as Anita got out of her field clothes and into off-matching office attire.

"This can't be how F.B.I. agents are selected." Anita queried.

"You are still in the army temporarily assigned to the F.B.I. I submitted your application for the academy."

"You know, little dude, if this F.B.I. thing of yours doesn't work out, you could get a job as a carnival huckster."

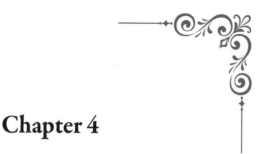

Chapter 4

"Sorry, we are late." Clarkson offered without even trying to mask the insincerity in his tone. "I was caught up in a game of name the Tyler with my staff."

There was a huge oval table with people from shoulder to shoulder and people standing behind them. There were people in various forms of dress, including military uniforms. Cameras had been set up as a sign that the meeting was being broadcast to people outside the conference room. The room had the feel that everyone was vying for their fair share of the oxygen, and an eyeballing competition was in play. Even with the hostility of the environment, the ugliest thing in the room was a giant picture of Flight 1317. Not the Airbus as it was rolled off the production line ten years ago, but the damaged mangles smattering of human remain saturated pieces that resulted in the event they were here to discuss.

The meeting barely began when the participants started lobbing insults and accusations at other departments. Anita found herself fixed on staring at the picture of the wreckage. Her mind overlayed the little boy rescuing the doll for the infant stranger. Anita was not clear on everything that was being said, but the terms accident and crash kept being used. Anita looked over at Clarkson and noticed him watching her. Clarkson did not like the F.B.I. character from some Hollywood movie; he looked more like a tired professor. Anita caught a sight nod from Clarkson. She now knew why she was brought here. And it was her turn to go all in.

"I know I am new here, but can we stop calling this an accident?" Anita's request had not been extremely loud, but it froze the room. It gave Anita the desired effect she had been looking for. Anita panned the faces of the others at the table, and a flood of information processed through for her.

"Director Cunningham, I disagree with junior associates in such a high-level meeting. No offense intended to Mr. Clarkson or Melody." A brass sound woman near the head of the table cried out.

There was murmuring and rumbling around the table. Anita was sure some of it was that old woman had been confused with Melody, whoever that was. Mrs. Clarkson had called her Mel during the phone conversation. This could be an explanation left for a better time.

A preppy-looking man with expensive dental work leaned over to an objected woman and began whispering something in her ear.

Ross Woodson was chairing the meeting, and Anita was aware she was the only one who did not know who he was in the packed room. Woodson leaned back in his chair with the prominence of Oden and spoke. "Well, let's not be so rash, Congresswoman; if the young woman has something to add to this meeting, let's hear it."

Anita looked at Clarkson, and he gave her a wink and a nod that let her off her lease.

"There was no crash. That plane was shot down. And by the looks on half the faces in this room, many of you knew it. It was just a matter of best informing the other half."

A grey-haired man in a General's uniform commanded. "Continue."

"Is she for real? Was that plane shot down over U.S. airspace, and the President has been informed?" The Congresswoman cried out.

"Who are you, and who do you represent." The preppy man with the Congresswoman asked in a snide tone.

"She is my newest assistant, and I might say in twenty minutes of looking at those photos, she spotted this crock of shit. How long do you think the national news will take to figure it out." Clarkson defended Anita.

"Maybe your new assistant can tell us the type of plane that shot down the aircraft." The general sarcastically stated.

Anita's anger got tangled in her enthusiasm as it sometimes did, and she walked over to the picture and pointed. "That is an entry hole, and the other side has an exit."

"So?" Woodson asked.

"Sir, I am sure the General gets my point. The shooter was on the ground, not in the air." Anita revealed.

A cold, eerie silence fell over the room. "It was a S.A.M., surface-to-air missile. A heat seeker. I went for the hottest point that would be the right engine."

"Is this your assessment too, Agent Clarkson?" Woodson asked.

"It is, but I have a question. Planes travel on routes. The old routes used to follow the train tracks." Clarkson walked slowly to where Anita was now standing. For the first time during the meeting, Anita was aware of the off-matching outfit she had been forced to wear. Others in the room noticed how Anita's ensemble had been haphazardly thrown together. "The questions and you can assume it to be rhetorical at this time, but why this flight? There would be easier flights shot down and others that could have caused more damage. But our shooter chose flight 1317; why?"

THE REMAINDER OF THE meeting was hostile at his brightest points and grossly combative at other times. When the meeting broke up, Harvey and Jerome ran to catch up with Anita and Clarkson.

"I don't know where you found her, but I'll take two." Harvey joked, looking at Anita.

"I only wish she had waited until Homeland started with one of those preposterous theories that John Q Public laps up. Like it was an explosion from a factory recall microwave that caused the plane to disintegrate before impact." Jerome joked.

"Bet that would be the last time anyone microwaved a bag of popcorn in a two-ton turbofan," Anita concluded.

Chapter 5

A nita woke up in a sweat. Her heart was racing, and she was apprehensive. Anita did not know how long she had been asleep, but it seemed like days. Clarkson had instructed Eric to book the team into a hotel near the crash site. Harvey and Jerome had agreed to give them a walking tour of the devastation. The team all got separate rooms, and Carolyn boasted of knowing the area and being willing to go shopping with Anita. With mild skepticism, Anita had agreed. That was Anita's first mistake. Carolyn's claim of knowing the area was exaggerated greatly, and it took a while to find decent shops that carried women's business suits. The shops where Carolyn knew carried women's attire more suited for clubbing. The second and most significant issue of having taken a shopping trip with Carolyn was that Carolyn flirted relentlessly. Carolyn flirted with young men, old men, single men, and men who were with what appeared to be their significant other.

Carolyn also chooses to attempt to correct Anita's speech. Anita is from Lamont, Mississippi, and is totally aware that she has an accent but did not approve of someone with you playing translator. Anita's discomfort seemed to go unnoticed by Carolyn.

Anita crossed the darkened hotel room; not sure she remembered the layout. She stumbled and almost fell on what she was looking for. It was her duffel bag. Anita dug into the duffle bag, throwing aside the contents until she found what she was searching for. It was a small, tattered, leather-bound bible that her mother had given her.

"Take this with you. You don't have to read it or even open it. But since it is a gift from me, a little piece of me will always be with you wherever you go," she could remember her mother telling her. Anita had been in the army for over two years and was used to sleeping in different places. It was not the strange surroundings or the awful shopping experience that had Anita in a sweat. The shopping trip had given him a bad dream. The bad dream catapulted her into a nightmare. She could see and hear the screams of the passengers from flight 1317. The children were calling for her help. "Oh God, I never meant to test your will, but are you sure? There are better people than me; hell, there are better Tylers than me. You are putting those babies in my heart. I am a smart-mouth poker-playing female quarterback." Anita whispered to herself. The only answer was a mile rain from outside the second-floor hotel room. Anita lies in the dark, hugging the bible and listening to the rain. She had her answer.

Chapter 6

A nita sat at a table at the Spencer Grand Hotel Coffee Shop, preparing for her breakfast. Clarkson had requested that she meet him in the coffee shop for breakfast. When Agent Clarkson came into the coffee shop, he handed Anita his cell phone, and Anita spoke briefly with Mrs. Clarkson. Mrs. Clarkson still seemed weak and drifted a little in her thought process, but her spirits seemed to lift talking to Anita, and Anita knew she could not deny Mrs. Clarkson that.

Agent Clarkson had taken back the phone and walked outside of Anita's hearing range to complete the phone conversation. When Agent Clarkson returned to the table, a short, stocky waitress appeared and laid a plate of food before him.

"Hey lady, what the hell is this." Clarkson bellowed, and the waitress tried to leave.

"It's your breakfast." The waitress answered in a snide tone.

Anita covered her mouth to keep from laughing.

"No. See, my breakfast is pancakes with blueberries and extra syrup and a big side of link sausages." Clarkson corrected. "This health-looking nonsense is someone else's. Some hippies, perhaps."

"Your daughter changed it while you were on the phone." The waitress was now getting agitated.

"Dad, please, you are making a scene. Have you taken your medication?" Anita had trouble keeping a straight face.

"She's not my daughter." Clarkson attempted to correct.

"Sure, she is. Why else would she put up with you? It would help if you were grateful your kid feels responsible for you. You have no idea how many people come in here with older relatives, and they treat them like dirt. She wants you to watch what you eat so she can keep you around a little longer and you act out." The waitress strutted off with a look of pride as if she had set at least one person right in this lifetime.

Clarkson gave Anita a deadly stare. But it was wasted on Anita she was now laughing at her handy work. "Here, this is a present for you. I picked it up on my shopping trip." Anita handed a small bag to Clarkson like a peace offering. Clarkson stopped picking at his vegetable omelet long enough to look in the bag. There were ties.

"Now see here, young lady. You work for me. I will not have you working as a spy for my wife."

"Men usually don't see the full effect of their ties on highlighting what they wear. I saw those, and they look like they would look good on you. I have no intention of stopping you from wearing those thrift store ties whenever you want."

Clarkson ate for a little and found he enjoyed the omelet and the whole wheat toast with peanut butter and banana more than he wanted to admit.

"Here, this is for you." Anita handed Clarkson some nicotine gum.

"Now look, people's habits are just that, personal."

"Yes, sir and I have no intent on campaigning for you to stop smoking, no matter how much I hope you do. But you probably know I am a good poker player since you know a lot about me.

"So."

Anita knew she had maneuvered him into a place where they could speak on a mutual level. "So yesterday in that conference, they asked you what you thought about what I was saying."

"Double so."

"So, you were fiddling with your hands. In poker people read tells on people. Subconscious hint or clues they are giving off."

"I know what a tell is, Agent Tyler."

Anita almost lost her train of thought, being called Agent Tyler. Eric called her that, but coming from Clarkson made it sound so official.

"Well, sometimes people accidentally or intentionally give off false tells. Some of the people there thought my speaking out was making you nervous. All the thing with your hand meant was that you wanted a cigarette."

Clarkson thought for a moment; he ate a little more than stated. "So, you are saying to work as a team, we need to cover each other's weaknesses and missteps, and you are ready to give me your best."

"Yes, and keep in mind we are your team. I may quarterback, but you are the coach."

Chapter 7

The rain subsided when Anita and Clarkson reached the crash site. Technicians from Harvey's team were everywhere. The workers had provided White coverings and hair bonnets for Anita and Clarkson. Harvey seemed anxious to get Clarkson alone to whisper some theory to him. Jerome took Clarkson's hint and began a tour for Anita. The wreckage recovery team worked feverishly and inspiringly professionally. Jerome seemed to be okay with the fact that some of the questions Anita asked were basic or had to be repeated for her to understand where one task connected to another fully. The team members were working to create a vector map for a holographic recreation of the event. Techs were graphing and mapping the location of parts to reconstruct the wreckage in an airplane hangar away from the elements.

Anita noticed that others she had seen briefly at the meeting were getting a tour of the site, but none as personal than what she and Clarkson had been offered.

"Harvey is good at what he does." Anita a point chose to comment.

"Harvey is the best. But it isn't just Harvey. Harvey inspires his people and strongly believes in training and positive reinforcement. People working for him don't feel like if they make a couple of mistakes or miss something, he is waiting to put them on an ice raft and set them afloat." Jerome commented.

"How do you deal with it? You are walking around of the lost hopes and dreams of over one hundred people?"

Jerome stopped and stared directly into Anita's eyes. "By knowing I cannot change what happened, but I damn sure can be a part of fixing it. Agent Tyler, that is where you and your boss come in. This was no accident. Find the bastards that did this, and don't let them breathe a second longer than it takes to track their asses."

Anita and Jerome notice a man headed directly for them. It took a moment for Anita to recognize him in a smock and bonnet, but it was the man with the overly expensive dental work from the meeting.

"Looks like someone wants a private word with you." Jerome noticed and started to wander back to some of his technicians.

Something caught Anita's attention. The ground was wet from the rain the night before. The entire area was farmland and woods. Anita, being from the south, knew the properties of farms. There was a technician pulling something from a shallow runoff. She knew runoff often appeared because water seeks its own level. The rain in the higher area was running down and filling the underground springs but at too fast a rate for the springs to accept the water, so the water would appear like a small creek for a short time.

"I must admit I find you intriguing. My name is Justin Albright. I am the executive assistant to Congresswoman Fletcher."

Anita barely noticed that the man who was headed for her had reached out and was talking to her. In the shallow temporary creek, a short female tech was putting something in a plastic bag that had been pulled from the creek. Anita broke out in a run that caught the attention of many of the people there. Anita grabbed the arm of the Technician and held her so she could examine what the woman was putting in the bag. It was a doll.

"Agent, if you need pictures and the catalog number for this, I can get it to you and your team." The female tech seemed almost frightened at the look on Anita's face.

"Do that." Anita requested, then noticed she still had a grip on the female Technician. As Anita released her grip, she noticed Justin had followed her.

"So now we know you are passionately into bloody, burned dolls; what do you say we get together later, Agent Tyler, and explore some of your other passions," Justin uttered in an over-rehearsed line of sleaze.

"Agent Tyler, are you alright." Eric had asked the question. He had noticed Anita sprinting across the field and had pursued her; only his speed was not as good as hers.

"Listen to me, you dime store Romeo. What the fuck would make even the most vile of dick weed think this was the appropriate time or place to troll for poon tang. Get away from me." Anita yelled into the face of Justin.

"Agent Tyler, I am about to help Homeland set up the three-D imaging diagram for the second site. Can you help me?" Eric asked.

Justin gave Eric a look that read he did not like being interrupted.

"Work. Remember. Burning babies falling from the sky. The reason we all came here." Anita snipped at Justin.

The distance between the two impact areas was greater than it seemed at first glance. The open field and the uphill made it look like the more you walked, the further away your destination got. Eric scampered to keep up with Anita; he was clearly not in the same physical condition she was. A Phalanx of news crews stood at the border of the restricted area of the telephoto lens cameras.

"Thank you." Anita finally slowed down before they reached the second group of tents and workers.

"For what?"

"Well, for one thing, you didn't jabber all the way up the hill. You gave me a chance to think."

"Yeah, there was that." Eric smiled.

"And you saved me from going maniac on the out-of-place playboy. Because you know I don't know rabbit shit about three D."

"No problem. The truth is, besides being in charge of I.T. for the team, I am also responsible for people with poor communication skills."

"Screw you."

"Yes, that is exactly what I mean."

They both got a chuckle out of Eric's deflection.

The site of the airplane engine was nothing short of epic. The hole going through the underside of the fan engine and mushrooming out through the other side is unmistakable. The large engine sat half-submersed in mud, looking like an abstract sculpture.

"I guess I should have known you were one of ours. The clown costume you wore to the meeting had me thrown for a bit." General Bradford walked up unnoticed and stood behind Eric and Anita.

"Sir, I take it you have been checking up on me. It seems like the local pastime."

"Just wondering what jackass would have the balls enough to back the room into a corner. Should have known it was army."

Anita wanted desperately to redirect the conversation. There was more here to see, and the General was an expert. "Handheld or vehicle mounted?" Anita asked.

"That depends. A handheld would do the trick. Commercial craft fly slow. This one had a cruising speed of 525 miles per hour. Some interceptors move three times that fast. Your plane was in landing mode, so it was slowing down." The General assessed. The General was a broad-shouldered man with an Acromegaly style chin and a deep, commanding voice. "Now I get the next question."

The general relaxed before asking. "How did you pull reassignment to the F.B.I. for temporary duty? I mean, just when I thought I had heard of every last dodge in the book."

"She is part of our summer intern program. Her application for Quantico is currently under review." Eric stated in a matter-of-fact tone. The General sneered and walked off.

"You should never lie to a general, young man," Anita said in a mock scolding voice.

"It was only half alive. One of those papers I had you sign while reading in the office was your application. Congratulations, welcome to the F.B.I." Anita watched Eric walk off to join a group of like-minded computer specialists, not knowing if he was serious or just attempting to one-up her for teasing him.

Chapter 8

The grandeur of the Spencer Grand Hotel had been deliberately understated. In fact, the grand design had been purposefully masked because it was the favorite hotel for businesspersons and government officials. The businesspeople and government officials flocked here for the same reason they did in hundreds of hotels in the U.S. and around the world: there were business resources readily available.

When Anita returned to the hotel, she was conflicted to the core of her being. She was used to being tired from maneuvers and exercises as a soldier. As a poker player and as the quarterback for a girls' team, she was used to being mentally stimulated to her fullest. Now, however, both sets of stimulation converged. It did not help that she was hungry. Carolyn had left with some other workers at the event site, returned with food, and set up a makeshift cafeteria, but no one had an appetite. Wandering through the lost lives that resonated throughout the valley stole their appetites.

Anita knew she had learned more than she could comprehend from the encounter. Clarkson had walked Anita around, explaining who all the dignitaries at the site were and how their jobs were interrelated. Most of the people Anita encountered were patriotically devoted to their causes, even when their patriotism was distorted by current pride or prejudice.

Anita found herself helpless to stop relentlessly teasing Eric the way she did her younger brothers. Eric did not seem to mind, even though he pretended to protest. Anita found the Eric had a talent for breaking down complicated computer operations in terms a layman could comprehend.

Carolyn took a turn to show Anita the workings of the operation. Still, she kept getting lost in flirting with workers who seemed more set in working the task. Carolyn suggested that she and Anita go on a double date with two of the men she knew from one of the agencies, and Anita knew it was time to stop Carolyn's portion of the training.

Anita wanted food and a drink. She spotted the hotel bar, and no sooner than she reached the doorway, she saw Justin holding court for a group of young women in the newspaper industry. Then Anita remembered that she had brought a bottle of Pettibone Brandy with her. It was a gift from her brother Lavon, who had received a crate of the brandy as thanks for saving a man's life. But she knew she had not opened the brandy because she had forgotten to put a corkscrew opener in her duffle bag. Anita saw a corkscrew opener on a serving table outside the bar and put it in her outer jacket pocket. Then Anita noticed a young man and woman staring at her. She wasn't stealing. She thought they could have their corkscrew opener back after she used it. Anita started walking toward the elevator to go to her room and noticed the Asian man and woman had started following her through the lobby. Anita turned to confront them, and another Asian couple appeared on her right. Anita clutched her purse where she had placed the Glock 9. There was no mistake in her reading of the four people converging on her; she was their target for whatever they had in mind.

"Miss Tyler, my superior would like a moment of your time." The smallest best dressed women of the group requested then look at Anita clutching the purse. "I assure you a shoot-out is not required." All the Asians seemed to join in a group smile session as the elevator opened, and there were already two very large Asian men in a suite in the elevator waiting for them.

"How could I resist?" Anita said in a smug tone.

The group squeezed into the elevator, and it began its ascent. When the door to the elevator opened on the penthouse floor, it was like Anita had stepped out of the elevator into not only a different hotel but a different world. Anita's room on the second floor was functional, but this area was lavish. An open design with a large picture window captured the early night skyline. Anita could see the light of a distant town or city on the horizon glowing like a hallow on the night sky. An Asian woman of a yet undeterminable age in a business suit stood staring at the sky. The woman's presence did not detract from the horizon's beauty but added to it.

Anita Tyler is thirty years old and 5'9 and has a good solid body frame. When the woman turned to face Anita, it was clear the woman was in her forties or fifties but had great physical makeup and was shorter than Anita.

"Welcome, Miss Tyler." The woman gestured Anita toward a seating area.

A game, good, I'll play, Anita thought, slowly walking toward the seats. The woman who had asked Anita into the elevator appeared rolling a cart with a tea service and Hors d'oeuvres.

The woman sat back in a chair facing Anita. The woman crossed her legs and, for a moment, seemed to be sizing up Anita.

"My name is Mai Li Chen. Please tell me how Waldren is?" The woman asked, then quickly pretended to correct. "I mean Agent Clarkson."

Anita noticed the woman's English was trained or taught English. Frequently, a homogenized form of English is taught when a person is taught English in a country where English is not the primary language. The persons teaching English may not know if you will speak with people from America, England, or Australia, all of whom speak English slightly differently—Anita's time in the army made her aware of what she was now hearing.

Anita smiled, noticed shrimp in the Hors d'oeuvres, and popped one into her mouth. She slowly chewed it and then threw another into her mouth. The female server poured tea for both Mai and Anita. Anita sipped her tea slowly and then answered. "So, we can keep this game fair. There are a few things I need to tell you about myself." Anita smiled, enjoying the attention of the people in the room. "First, I am a hell of a poker player. I read tells like you would not believe. But more importantly I read false tells better than most people."

"And what does this have to do with our conversation?" Mai Li was seriously confused.

"Well, if we were playing Texas Holdem, I would almost feel bad about taking your money. Almost. You are projecting tells all over the place."

"Perhaps for my edification, you should explain what these tell are?" Mai Li asked, looking at her associates as if they held the answer.

"Well, a tell is a subconscious clue that someone broadcast that gives away the strength of their hand."

"And in the short time you have been in this room, what have I broadcasted?" Now, Mai Li was intrigued.

"You deliberately referred to my boss as Waldren while referring to me as Miss Tyler. You wanted me to know that you know him personally. But you did not want to tell me that unless I asked. Your eyes fell as if preparing for bad news when I did not answer immediately. That is a concern. You like him. Maybe you two are not on the best of terms right now, but if it is up to you, you would patch things up right away." Anita stopped and downed some more food. "How am I doing so far?"

Mai Li looked a way, as the cloak of embarrassment could not hide how spot-on Anita was. Mai Li looked around the room at her associates, who brought Anita to the penthouse. "I think I must learn this game of poker. I have heard of it, but it seemed so useless until now."

"What I don't know is what you brought me here to tell me or show me."

"Oolong tea." Mai Li looked into her cup.

Anita was unsure, but there was a message here, and she needed more time to figure out riddles. Anita stood and started walking toward the elevator. "Thank you for the oblong tea."

Mai Li ran to Anita before she could enter the elevator and put something in Anita's purse. Anita knew whatever Mai Li had slipped into her purse was the most critical part of the meeting. Anita couldn't be sure, but it was as if the people who were guarding Mai Li were also keeping some part of her prisoner. But for now, she was fatigued and needed the nightcap she had planned.

ANITA GOT IN THE ELEVATOR alone in the penthouse and pressed two for her floor. The elevator stopped at six, and two men got on. One of the men was large, like a football player or bodybuilder, and had a buzz cut. The other man was dark-haired and about Anita's height. As soon as the door to the elevator closed on the sixth floor, the big man motioned himself behind Anita and put his arm across her throat with his massive forearm. Buzz cut began choking Anita in such a way that she was lifted off the floor. Anita started struggling to get the gun from her purse, but the dark-haired man knocked the purse from her hand. She was choking and in fear of losing her life, but it was not her possible impending death that motivated her. It was the cries of the children of Flight 1317. Anita knew the most dangerous thing in a life-or-death situation was to give up. The dark-haired man turned around to hit the stop button on the elevator, and Anita reached into her jacket pocket. There was the corkscrew opener she had pilfered. Quickly, Anita measured where Buzz Cut's head was touching her just behind her head and jabbed the pointed side of the opener in a hard single motion. There was no mistake that she had found the target.

Buzz Cut screamed and grabbed his eye or what was left of it. The dark-haired man turned around immediately and, grabbed Anita's neck with one hand and went for a pistol in his belt with the other. In his haste, the dark-haired man did not realize Anita still had the corkscrew opener until she jabbed him in the neck; Anita, at the same time, grabbed the man's hand as he went for the gun, and instead of trying to wrestle it from him, squeezed his hand causing the gun to fire before clearing his pants. Both men were bloody and screaming in a European Language. Anita had no idea what it was.

Anita hit the button for the elevator to resume and then resumed stabbing the men. Anita fell back against the elevator door, and as it opened, she fell backward on the floor. She scrambled to retrieve her gun and badge. Anita crawled from the elevator, bloody and shaking. An older couple was waiting for the elevator, dressed for an evening out. The old woman began screaming, and the old man started yelling for security.

Finally, the lady stopped screaming when she saw security arriving. "Gee, can somebody call my boss? He is on the fifth floor; his name is Clarkson. This is my first week on the job, and I really hope I ain't in too much trouble."

Chapter 9

"Are you thinking the same thing I am?" Clarkson asks Anita. Anita sat in the rear doorway of a paramedic vehicle while a female paramedic checked her for serious injury.

"God, I hope not. I was thinking no matter what that fat lady says in those commercials about this bra still being confrontable after 12 hours, that's a load of horseshit. This thing is really starting to bite. I need to go to my room and let the girls fly free, so to speak."

"A no would have sufficed, Agent Tyler."

The paramedic could not help but laugh and then walked out of hearing range to maintain professionalism.

"My boss thinks I am losing my mind putting an untrained agent into what may be the most significant case of the decade."

"Please don't pull me, coach. Don't you see it? There must be four dozen teams working on this mess right now from God knows how many agencies. But the one person they want out of the way is the newest. The one who should know the least and present the least threat." Anita looked at Clarkson with her serious side exposed for the moment.

"That was the answer you were supposed to give me before."

"Yeah, but what would have been the fun in that."

"HERE IS YOUR PURSE." Eric had also been concerned when he heard that Anita had been attacked on the elevator. A crowd of confused spectators was starting to dissipate, and Anita remembered something. Anita reached into her purse to find what Mai Li had placed there. It was a picture of a man with Asian features in a military uniform. "How long would it take for you to find out who this is?"

"It's not a magic act that I do, but I can check it out. If any of the agencies we are working with know who this is, it won't take but a couple of hours. The only downside is every agency we are working with will know we want to know who he is?" Eric was about 5'6" and had a small frame, but he knew the craft they were working with well and knew it was his job to keep her aware.

"Do it anyway.

Chapter 10

It was slightly after midnight, a day that showed no sign of ending when Eric knocked on the door. Eric was carrying a laptop and a computer bag and pushed himself into the room the minute she opened it. Anita had showered and was wearing a robe; she had washed the blood and stench from her hair and wrapped it in a towel.

"I found your guy. It was easier than I thought, but I did not want it to wait until morning under the circumstances." Eric plopped down on the small half sofa in the room, pulled up the coffee table, and began unpacking his gear. Eric did not explain what he meant by, under the circumstances, but it was clear he felt Anita was making him a part of a conspiracy against their boss.

"So, who is he, and what's the big deal?" Anita paced.

"He got on the plane as Lee Chu. That's how we found him. Homeland oversees TSA. After the plane went down, they pulled all photos of anyone at TSA check-in and cross-matched with anyone getting on the plane."

"So, if I understand you correctly, Lee Chu was on the plane that went down?"

"No."

"Come again."

"Lee Chu is Chinese Intelligence for John Smith. I crossed this guy with the Chinese embassy, and there is a better than 80 percent match. He is John Chen, a Chinese intelligence agent. We are relying on facial recognition software. Despite what you see on crappy tv shows, facial recognition software is not perfect. It does not work as well on some races or facial types as on others. What we do know is that the person who checked in at TSA processing and the guy who got on the plane and was blown to bits was the same guy. We believe it was John Chen."

"Who the fuck would blow up a whole plane to kill one spy?"

"Maybe the same people that would send a couple of Bosnian hitmen for a meet and greet on an elevator. Look, I got to bring the boss in on what we know in the morning. You have to fess up about how you got the picture."

"How do you know I did not already tell him?"

"I think I am starting to get your style, Agent Tyler."

Anita smiled, thinking how much Eric reminded her of home. "You know you remind me of Noreen, my little sister,"

"Remember I said I was responsible for helping with crappy communication skills? Just a tip about how to get along with male coworkers. Never tell them they remind you of your little sister."

Before either could decide if they were going to laugh, there was a soft know on the door.

"You, expecting someone?" Eric asked.

"No, but I really wasn't expecting anyone in the elevator either. But holly shit, there they were."

"Try not to stay up late. We have a rendezvous in the morning." Eric stated, collecting his gear.

"Back to the crash site?"

"No, we got vectors on where the rocket came from. Carolyn has arranged for the local FBI swat team to lead us in."

"Does this job get easier?" Anita asked, opening the door, and Mai Li was standing there. "I guess not."

Anita stared at Mai Li for a moment, saying nothing. Mai Li looked different from the confident woman she had projected only a few hours before. Mai Li stood alone, but Anita knew Mai Li's entourage was nearby.

"If you came to kick my ass, you are too late. besides, I have help now." Anita gave Eric a hearty slap on the back.

"I only came to talk privately, woman to woman." Mai Li offered.

"Alright, little dude, that means you are out of here. Besides, I know your big brain could use some rest."

"I got a couple of things to check out anyway. Remember, honesty is the best policy." And with this, Eric was off.

Chapter 11

Mai Li entered the room and sat precisely where Eric had been seated. Anita left the room and quickly returned with two hotel glasses and the bottle of brandy she had opened to breathe before Eric arrived. Anita poured two glasses and then gave one to Mai Li.

"Sorry, but my room is not as nice as your suite, and I am all out of oblong tea."

Mai Li giggled a little for the first time, and something other than the game they were playing revealed itself. "Oolong." Mai Li corrected and took a drink of the brandy. Surprise filled her eyes, suggesting great pleasure. "There are places in the east that you would pay a king's ransom for even rot gut whiskey, which is American. This is excellent." Mai Li offered presenting her glass for a refill.

"This is good stuff. My brother Lavon sent me a bottle. Some gangster's daughter gave it to him. He is a cop in some one-horse town."

"Why only one horse allowed." Anita was still determining if Mai Li was joking or had limited knowledge of American expression. Mai Li's English was clear and crisp, no doubt of professional training. "I came to apologize."

Anita smiled and drank.

"What are you reading in me now, Agent Tyler?"

"That you gave me the photo because you wanted closure. The young man in the picture is someone very special to you, and you had to know for sure if there was even a remote chance he was not on that plane."

"Your gift makes you a natural for this line of work."

"He has your eyes and coloring. If I were to guess, he is a relative of yours. Since you did not want even your staff to know you were desperate to find out if he is still alive, he is or was your son."

"I have got to learn this game of poker." Mai Li stated in a weak voice. "Then you know he was on the flight 1317?"

"We believe so. But since we are putting our cards on the table, so to speak. Why?"

"Why, what?"

"I might be new at this, but I am pretty sure Clearmont is not on the list of Chinese must-see stops, for when you get to America, I damn sure know Portland is not. So, it's like someone telling you they saw the queen of England in the local Shop for Less."

"Can I assume by your question you know what line of work my son was involved in?"

"Chinese State Security Ministry, I will hazard guessing."

"You are learning much in a short time, Agent Tyler. Do not let it be your downfall."

"Is that a threat?"

"No, a warning. Woman to woman." Mai Li stood to leave.

"One more thing before you go. What is the deal between you and my boss?"

The room was silent for a moment as Mai Li sifted her thoughts for a way to answer Anita's question. "We were friends and very close. Our friendship had nothing to do with our work, or so we thought. One day, someone told me I had to deceive Waldren on a matter important then but of no consequence these days."

"So, you had to lie to him or withhold information you knew he needed?" Anita confirmed.

"He found out and did the one thing that hurt me the most."

Anita waited for the next comment to fall.

"He forgave me and told me he understood."

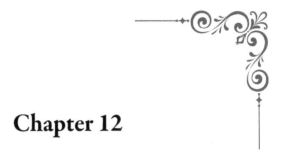

Chapter 12

Anita sat in the rear seat beside Agent Clarkson. I picked up two assault vehicles from the FBI after breakfast. The FBI swat team was Hatcher, the team leader, Cook, Graham, Logan, and Wentworth. Anita and Clarkson sat in the back of one vehicle. At the same time, Hatcher drove, and the others piled into the second vehicle. Anita was sure the seating arrangement was not by accident. She knew Clarkson wanted to scold her. Clarkson had a healthy breakfast this time without complaining. He insisted that Anita spoke to his wife on the phone again and restricted his comment to Anita to one-word answers for the morning. Anita looked down at Clarkson's hands and noticed him fidgeting. Clarkson saw Anita staring and popped one of the pieces of nicotine gum in his mouth.

"How are the men from the elevator?" Anita finally began the conversation.

"Let's see. The one you stabbed in the neck and shot in the dick is touch and go." Clarkson began.

"Gee, if you shot some guy's dick off, he might not care if he pulls through," Hatcher commented from the front seat. Hatcher was a big, strong, broad-shouldered, and broad-chested man. The type of man you could not imagine wearing some form of uniform.

"Do you mind we are trying to have a private conversation," Clarkson noted before continuing. "The other guy won't speak English, but I am pretty sure he is saying either I want my eye back or can you tell her to bring my eye back? My Bosnian is a little rusty."

Anita tried with all her might not to laugh. "Look, boss, I know you are mad at me."

"Agent Tyler, you met with a foreign intelligence official on U.S. soil and did not inform your superior. It was only yesterday that you gave me the Coach versus Quarterback speech."

"First, let me apologize for the delay in telling you. The only thing Mai Li asked of any importance was how you were doing these days. It sounded personal. She referred to you by first name. It did not sound like the best thing to put in a report. As for taking the meeting, I was forced into the elevator by a gang of the best dress Thugs I have ever seen." Anita slipped back into the seat before continuing. "She stopped by the room after the elevator incident for a nightcap and to apologize for giving me the picture and putting my life in danger."

"What do we know about the man in the picture?"

"I am sure he was her son. A mother deserves closure doesn't sound like something that goes in a report either."

A wave of sadness washed over Clarkson's face that was hard for Anita to understand completely. "Then there is the other little problem."

Clarkson braced for more bad news.

"I have played in many poker tournaments, and I have even been involved in setting up a couple. Sometimes, we need an area as large as that penthouse."

"So."

"So those rooms are booked in advance. She knew where I was going to be long before I did. Eric says he is working on an angle for something that does not fit about this mess."

Clarkson now looked like the man with the schoolteacher demeanor again. "I am sorry I did not tell you I know your father. A long time ago, your father and I had a long talk about raising daughters." Clarkson began.

"I guess you straighten him out," Anita stated.

"No, he was the one with the wisdom. Considering how many daughters he has; I should have just shut up and listened. One thing he said that keeps playing in my mind recently is that every father says you must be sure not to break your son's spirit if you want him to grow up to be a strong, independent man. It works the same for girls to become strong, independent women. Anita, it is not my plan to break your spirit."

"If you are calling me spirited, I think I like that a lot more than what I have been calling myself lately." Anita confessed, "Coach, I don't care how much we fight. I want those bastards."

In the conversation as in physical time and space they had reached their appointed destination.

Chapter 13

"Alright, the way it works is I have tactical command, so you spies will take a rest break here. No sooner than those pencil-neck geeks calculated the launch site for our killer rocket, Homeland had the good sense to declare the whole area a no-fly zone. So, any pictures of the area are hours old. The last pic we got was from the park ranger helicopter, and it might as well have been a cave painting. We go in to clear the area and then bring you geniuses in. That way, no one accidentally gets his dick shot off." Hatcher stated with complete authority in his voice. The group split up near a bunch of trees where Clarkson and his team could watch and still be out of the line of fire. The area consisted of two buildings. One building was an old farmhouse, exactly as expected for the area.

The second building looked like a large barn, but there was no evidence of what purpose the barn served. There were no food or watering stations for animals and no production equipment.

"How come you got to ride with the cute guy Hatcher?" Carolyn asked, moving up behind Anita and watching the FBI swat team move down the hill toward the farmhouse.

"Carolyn, you got to ride with three cute guys, including Eric."

"Well, I guess so, but did he ask you anything about me?"

Without answering, Anita walked over and stood behind Eric, who was watching the Swat team approach through binoculars.

"Are you mad at me?" Eric asked without looking around at Anita.

"A friend should never get mad at you for doing what you should, Eric. And a real friend should never try to get you to compromise who and what you are for their own purposes." Anita looked back over her shoulder at Carolyn.

"Thank you, Agent Tyler. I guess I needed to hear a female say that."

AS SOON AS THE SWAT team was within 25 feet of the barn, there was an automatic hiss, and a red laser beam flashed toward the swat team. The swat team dived for the ground, and a volley of automatic machine gun fire sounded. There was a whirling and clicking associated with an electric Gatling gun on a turret.

"Stay where you are. Let the gun run out of rounds. It is robotic. There is no human. It's a bobby trap." Eric yelled into a walkie-talkie.

"WHAT THE HELL IS THAT thing anyway?" Clarkson asked as his team joined the battered Swat team. Hatcher kept examining the shooting system that had almost cut his team in half. There were numerous minor injuries, but luckily, due to a safe, cautious approach, there were no deaths.

"A ghost gun?" Hatcher answered.

"What does that mean?" Anita asked.

"It means there is no serial number or logo anywhere on this thing. It looks like an M61-A2 set to fire 6000 plus rounds in a minute, but it is too small and light." Hatcher answered, still examining the gun.

"I got the tech team on the way for pictures, prints, and process of the place; who is up for a look-see in the barn?" Carolyn asked.

"What branch of our government did it come from?" Anita clarified her question.

"I did not come from our government. We own no such animal." Hatcher explained.

Clarkson's team began staring at each other, hesitating about what they would find in the barn.

THE BARN WASN'T MUCH of a barn at all. There was a large open space and worktables. There was a machining lathe and a few tools. There was a 55-gallon drum in the room with ash where documents had been burned to ash. Eric noticed a small strip of paper caught beneath the barrel, retrieved it, and put it in a plastic bag. It was part of a receipt. The name of the company and the zip code were the only thing he could make out.

After a little work on his computer, he found what he was looking for: a Miller Machine Tool and Die in Boseman, Montana.

"Carlyon, get us on the first plane out of here to Boseman," Clarkson ordered.

"Enjoy your flight." Hatcher offered.

"No such luck, young man. I still have you assigned to me, you and your crew or with us."

"Jesus, fricking Christ, what the hell is even in Boseman?" Hatcher complained.

Chapter 14

The flight was bumpy and uncomfortable, but Anita loved it. Carolyn could not get into a commercial fight fast enough, so she hitched a ride with an Air Force cargo plane. Anita felt like progress was being made. Clarkson did not wait for approval or endless discussions with his boss. He followed the trail.

Two swat team members, Logan, and Wentworth, were arguing about who would win the college divisional football game for the region they came from.

"I'll tell you what, I'll get you a hundred dollars. The quarterback Hammond smokes Regan." Logan finally proposed.

"Anita laughed, and the swat team seated across from her team all stopped and stared at her."

"What is so funny, Agent?" Logan asked.

"The bet. Hammond is going to lose big time." Anita answered.

Now, both groups were watching her, waiting for her reasoning.

"Look, Hammond has the better record 8 and 3," Logan said with mild agitation and a dash of gender-driven pomposity.

"Would you like for me to explain why?" Anita queried.

"Go for it. No offense but women don't know dick about football." Wentworth commented.

Anita accepted the challenge. "Hammond is a warm-weather quarterback. He can't throw the ball any better than one of my little sisters on a day that is below 40 degrees. He has the better record because his schedule has him in warm places at the beginning of the season. Didn't you notice how crappy he was at the end of his last game? That was because the weather started to drop. Any real coach would have pulled him to protect the lead. But he is such a baby they don't want to deal with temper tantrums this late in the season."

"You sound like you played a little yourself." Cook, the group's female, noticed and was now interested in the conversation.

"Yeah, I'm a quarterback for the girls' church league back home. We are mostly a way to raise funds for the poor, but we take it serous enough. I also Quarterbacked in the women's army games."

"How did you do against the marine's women?" Hatcher asked, pulled into the conversation.

"We won the first two and lost the last one, but I think they need to chromosome or steroid test some of their horses."

This caused a big round of laughter.

"Where about you from, country girl," Cook asked.

"Lamont Mississippi."

"What do you like about being the quarterback?" Cook asked.

Before answering, Anita looked at Clarkson, who seemed intrigued even if he was not part of the conversation. She realized he may know her father, but he did not know her. He had taken a lot of faith, and she had to live up to it as best she could. "My brother Norbert taught me to throw the ball. He said no sister of mine is going to embarrass the shit out of me throwing like a girl." This caused more laughter. "I like reading the defense, knowing what they are thinking and what they are capable of. I like knowing my team. I knowing who is having a bad day and who is set to have the game of their lives. I love that they trust me to put this all-in motion without regard for my person."

"Do you play with guys or girls or mixed?" Cook asked.

"I play flag mixed, guys and girls. When I play girls only, I pay either flag or tackle."

"Afraid the boys will get rough." Logan taunted.

"It's not that exactly. You see when you outplay or maneuver some people, male or female, their feelings can get crushed. I don't want someone bigger and stronger than me tackling me long after the play has gone dead because their feelings are bruised."

"Guys can be brutes." Cook chimed in.

"Yes, they can be, but it is not always their fault. It is how they are brought up. My sister Jody is a female bodybuilder, and she can wrestle around with the best of guys. I have seen her tackle girls in a flag game out of enthusiasm. I also have seven brothers, some of the biggest boneheads God had the grace to place on this earth. And I know if they hurt some poor girl quarterback in a moment of bad choices or having lost their temper for a split second, they would feel really bad themselves."

"You aren't by chance related to a jackass by the name of Lavon Tyler, are you?" Hatcher asked. "Seminole football player a few years back."

"That's one of my brothers. Do you know him?"

"No, but I played in that game where he played offense and defense. The guy was unstoppable."

"He still is. He's a cop now."

Anita switched seats and sat next to Clarkson. "I am so sorry if I screwed up boss."

"No, Agent Tyler, no reason to be sorry. I should have known Mai Li had the decency to want to help even if she was afraid to approach me directly."

"If Chinese intel is trying to come to our rescue, does that mean this mess is worse than one downed plane with over one hundred dead bodies?"

"I am afraid it is far worse."

Anita was unsure if she was out of questions or too afraid to hear possible answers, so she left it at that.

Chapter 15

Once on the ground, the Clarkson's team went to work. Carolyn found them a cheap motel to set up, the best that could be done on such short notice. Carolyn had contacted the local FBI office for assistance and warrants for the Miller Manufacturing plant search were underway.

Eric, a little sick from motion sickness from the flight, began running record checks on the workers as best he could. He then checked public tax records and ownership papers for the plant.

Anita had gone to her assigned room and lay on the bed looking at the ceiling while she tried to make sense of the swirling mess in front of her. Just before a mental bog of self-doubt could suck under Anita, there was a knock on her room door; it was Eric.

"Okay, so you started me thinking with that statement about who would shoot down an entire plane for one spy. One junior spy at that." Eric was still in a little pain, but whatever he had found was rushing him back to health. Eric put his laptop on the bed and began opening up information. "Our Chinese spy was following someone. Poor guy probably had no idea how important the person he was following was to someone."

"Who and how do you know?"

"Because this is what I do for a living. Remember that the next time you decide to compare me to your little sister."

"I said I was sorry, so keep going."

"I had friends run the Lee Chu alias at hotels, car rentals and restaurants for the Clearmont area. I then took the list from Homeland on who was on the plane and did the same search. I had the computer cross-reference the two lists. There was only one match, Bryan Sheldon."

"Bryan Sheldon, the writer?"

"The same."

All the pity and self-doubt of moments before evaporated; this was going somewhere, and Anita now knew it.

"So, what is the next play quarterback?" Eric asked.

"I am walking a thin line between hero and villain with the boss. Are you sure you want direction from me?"

Eric turned and faced Anita. He looked at her with the most serious look she had ever seen on his face. "Whoever these people are, they kill without a moment of hesitation; if only one of us has the information, there is a good chance it dies with us. We have to double down."

"Deal. By the way, what is with you and Carolyn?"

Eric thought for a moment. "We went out a few times when she first joined the team. She believes at her age and this point in her life, she does not feel she should limit herself to one guy."

Anita was conflicted; in one way, she was sorry she had asked, but now so much made sense regarding the way the two interacted.

"I know there are a lot of people my age that play the game. But I can't be with a girl that I know sleeps around."

Anita now knew more than ever about Eric and how he views personal relations in his life. The big sister in her wanted to tell him he would someday find a girl who appreciated his value system. But Anita was afraid she might overstep the rights of a new friendship. And who was she kidding? After the case, she would be back in uniform in the army, waiting for her release date.

"Alright, you clowns, the warrant is here. Let's go meet some manufacturing people." Clarkson pounded on the door, rallying his troops.

Chapter 16

"What exactly do you produce here, ma'am?" Clarkson now stood in the office of the head of production for the Miller Manufacturing Facility. The woman was Ida Rosenstein. She was a pale, thin middle-aged woman with greying hair. Ida's fingers were long and narrow, and the tips were burned and calloused from holding unfiltered cigarettes to the last possible moment of her enjoyment. The office was cluttered with books, records, and files in such an array that it made it look like a junk closet after a heavy windstorm. There were also bins of metal parts that were the inner workings of God only knows what. There was an overpowering smell of stale cigarette smoke past, present, and, if possible, the future. In front of Ida on her desk was a large round ask tray filled to the overflow with cigarette butts and ash. Competing and doing a fair job with the nauseating smell of carcinogens was the smell of solvent, oil-based cutting solution, and water-based cutting solution.

"Produce. What kind of idiot are you? Big government trying to control everybody and everything and don't have a rats ass clue to what they are doing. You got a fucking warrant, and you don't know what we do?" Angrily the old production supervisor stared at Clarkson, then continued her rant. "And by the way, aren't you a little old for this job? I mean, the FBI guys on TV are a lot younger and a hell of a lot better looking. I guess that's why you travel with such a young group to do the work. That's the problem with America today. Too many old farts willing to let their kid carry them the rest of the way to the grave."

Anita stood beside Clarkson, watching the anger mount in his face. Anita had not known Clarkson long enough to know everything about him. Still, he was starting to remind her more and more of her father, and she knew that if Clarkson erupted, it would not be good for anyone.

"With all due respect, they don't produce a finished product, boss. They produce precision metal components for various devices. Clocks, transmissions, guns, you name it, if the metal device's inner workings must work the same every time, is what they specialize in.

"This kid is a keeper. Got a good head on her shoulders. Would have taken me half an hour to explain that to you." Ida sneered.

"Quarterback, you got the ball." Clarkson turned and walked out of the room.

Chapter 17

The night had fallen, and Anita had found Clarkson. Clarkson was in the bar at Deluxe Motel, where the team was staying. This motel was shabby not only compared to the hotel where the group had stayed in Portland but also in comparison to what Bozeman had to offer in general.

The search of the Miller facility had gone well. Eric had accessed the company computer system and found a treasure trove of interesting information.

Carolyn found accounting anomalies in the accounting department, usually associated with tax evasion, and called the IRS with Anita's permission. The IRS arrived with their team in a couple of hours, sent the worker home, and padlocked the place. This was primarily because Miller had several government contacts to produce some parts, and the contacts were clear on how the government would handle fraud, misrepresentation, and tax evasion.

Even the Swat team got plenty of work. Fortunately, there were no robot-driven electric machine guns to duck. Still, they assisted in tasks like coping files and questioning employees. Ida, the production manager, and her supervisors were the only Caucasian employees at Miller. All of Miller's other employees were black or Hispanic. A few of the Hispanic employees tried to pretend they needed to speak clear English during questioning, which failed miserably in the Spanish was Swat Team member Logan's first language, and he was happy to translate.

"Thank you for today. It would have taken me all week to do what you put in motion today." Clarkson said without turning to look at Anita as she walked up. A sad song was being sung in the jukebox in Spanish, and Clarkson sat with a lonely stare into the whiskey glass in front of him. Anita ordered beer and sat down at the bar next to him.

"Don't be so quick to thank me. I need two things, depending on how much you trust me."

"Why do I feel like I am about to make a deal with the devil?"

Anita ignored the comment and made the first request. "The next time Mai Li contacts me, I want your permission to talk to her."

"You had a good day, Agent Tyler. Hell, you had a great day. But you are not physic. You cannot guess that she will come around asking questions."

"I can because I read my father's book 'The Soft Touch of Conversion,' and I know the two people that fell in love with his book were you and Mai Li." Anita took no pride in her revelations, only sadness that the conversation could not go any further without her revealing what she had surmised thus far.

"It was a mistake I made long before you were born."

"Whatever you do, don't tell her you think loving her was a mistake, no matter what. Because she still loves you, I could see it in her face. And I said a mother needs closure, as does a father."

Clarkson turned and looked at Anita. "What are you proposing."

"John Chen was most likely your son. And you know it. Before you try to convince yourself, it is false, let me lay down a few more of my cards. First, you got mad at me and could have sent me packing, but you had to know what I knew and had figured out. Next, consider your work in the FBI. But not only the FBI, the division that handles national threats, but you had no clue you had an out-of-wedlock child by a Chinese spy. That is because she had to hide it from you and everyone else. Her child would have been a prime target to use in some form of infiltration capacity. But his mother got him the lowest of assignments. She was hiding him from you and her government by hiding him right under their noses."

"When I sat with your father and gave him the story, I begged him to leave out much of the detail. When you are young, you think the rules don't apply to you. By the time you find out they do, there is always a mess. Some people spend the second part of their lives cleaning up the messes they made in the first." Clarkson seemed relieved to be able to talk to someone about this. Like a million men in this world, at his age, his wife was not only his spouse but also his best friend, and where does a man go with secrets he dares not share with his best friend?

"A long time ago, my father was on some manhunt for a dangerous killer. One of those, you will never take me alive types. My mother tried not to seem worried, but all the kids knew she was. One evening after church, all of us children gathered together and made a deal with each other and with God. That is, if he brought my father back home to Mom, we would all do something in our lives to help others." Anita explained as much to herself as to Clarkson.

"So, you have been staring at the children in that photo, wondering if god came to collect his end of the bargain?" Clarkson concluded.

"I did not come here to blame you for things you did long before I was born. I only want your permission to hear her out if she shows up to talk about the wonderful child her son was before some bastard blew him up."

Anita signaled for another beer, and the two sat briefly without speaking until Clarkson stated. "You said there were two things."

"Yes, I need your permission to have Eric set up a teleconference meeting with the New York branch of the FBI. I need the meeting set up a special way so I can read tells."

"Permission granted. You know, the one thing no one tells you about getting older is that your world starts to shrink." Clarkson looked deeply into the remainder of his drink. "But one good thing out of today for me is that after the visit to the angry little chain smoker's office, it may be a while before I want another cigarette. Permission granted, Agent Tyler, despite what this mess is doing to us all personally, I think we are making progress."

Chapter 18

Eric had the New York FBI office linked with the Bozeman office via a secured satellite link. The New York Director and Director Cunningham, Clarkson's boss, insisted on being allowed into the meeting on a blind feed, which meant the people being interviewed had no clue they were there listening in. Eric and Anita ensured Anita and Clarkson could always see the two people being interviewed and that they could watch body motions and facial expressions. The woman being interviewed was Rachel Galloway, the agent of record for the late Bryan Sheldon, and Hadley Peterson, a lawyer who had come in the event that a consul was needed for Ms. Galloway. Anita also ensured that Galloway and Peterson could see her and Clarkson for her plan to work.

"Agents Clarkson and Tyler, how can we help the FBI today?" This was the first question Peterson asked after the introductions.

"Do you love this country?" Clarkson asked.

"Excuse me?" Peterson asked.

"Simple question: do you love this country? Let me make it clearer: do you love freedom?"

"Look, I don't know what you are selling, but yes, I love this country," Peterson answered. Peterson was a young man who looked like if you woke him in the middle of the night, he would be wearing a three-piece suit.

"What about you, Ms. Galloway? Do you love this country? And do you know what the penalty for treason is?"

"What," Galloway screamed.

"Simple question: hundreds of dead and an act of terrorism covered under the Patriot Act." Just as planned, Clarkson threw the first volley to disorientate his prey.

"Terrorism, you mean the plane that Sheldon was on. Oh god, the news is starting to say the plane had exploded before hitting the ground." Galloway stared at Peterson.

"Are you Mirandizing Ms. Galloway currently? Is she under arrest?"

Clarkson gave Anita the nod, wink, and put a piece of the nicotine gum in his mouth. Anita knew her cue.

"Ms. Galloway, please understand my boss. He is not only an old-line patriot who has served this country all his life. But also, a family man. The thought of anyone withholding information that would help the FBI arrest a mass murderer is appalling to him."

Galloway looked like a woman drowning in an ocean and had seen a raft. All she wanted was for someone to throw her a little rope.

"Now I have a question," Anita said, standing and picking up a piece of paper from the desk in front of her. The paper was the Chinese takeout menu for delivery to the neighborhood, but she was sure the interviewees had no clue what she was reading.

"I don't recommend my client answers any more questions at this time," Peterson stated.

"Good, just as well. Because the next question was for you, my sister works in criminal law. What type of law is it? That say, it is your specialty?" Anita stared down at the menu.

Peterson swallowed so hard you could hear it. His eyes darted about like all he wanted was out of this room. "Copyright and patent infringements." He dryly confessed.

"So, if I am clear, you would like for us to stop the interview so you can get Ms. Galloway connected to a lawyer more familiar with treason and lethal injection."

Galloway sprang to her feet. "Whoa, lady, hold the fuck on. I don't get a big enough cut of what these guys get to get injected. A freaking nine-million-dollar deal, and my cut is peanuts in comparison to what others are getting from this project."

Peterson stared to mumble something, but Galloway cut him off. "Shut up, you are fired. What do you need to know?"

"Well, maybe I did one too many pushups in the army, but it looks like Sheldon has a clone. He was working on a movie screenplay in one place and releasing a book on the other side of the country at the same time. How could that be." Anita flipped the menu over to check out the soups.

"Alright, Sheldon's name sells the books. He has a ghostwriter that does most of the work. Sheldon gets so drunk the minute the check gets in his hand he is unusable, sometimes for months. The ghost is in Portland."

Clarkson sat up at attention so quickly you could almost hear the alarm bell go off in his head.

"ANYBODY WANT TO TELL me what I just witnessed before someone reads me my rights." Director Hunter of the New York office asked if the feed to the interviewee had been severed.

"Agent Tyler, will you do the honors." Clarkson offered.

"Certainly, sir, you see, I come from a family with fourteen kids, and my mom used to be a schoolteacher. All the neighborhood kids would sometimes gather at our house." Anita began. "Noreen was the best at most games. She was the most logical mind of the group. Jody hated a lot of the games we would play on rainy days. We call her the Bull in a China Shop 'cause she is so rough; she would rather be somewhere lifting something heavy any day of the week."

"Please promise me there is an explanation in here somewhere." Director Cunningham, Clarkson's boss, requested.

"Well, yes, sir, there is. See, my mom had a game she would play with us on rainy days. She collected these puzzles. She would put them in bags and shake the bag. She hides the box with the picture of what it was supposed to look like when it was finished."

"So," Hunter stated.

"Well, sir, don't you get it? Someone is shipping parts like puzzle pieces all over the place for weapons like the electric Gatling gun that the swat team encountered. To close off any loose ends, they kill the assembly team when they are no longer needed."

"Okay, so wait a minute, you are saying they aren't smuggling weapons. There are smuggling parts to be reassembled. And they can build a launcher that shoots down a jet. Don't weapon like these need computer components and chemical compounds to operate."

" After our forensic analysis, you will find that the software they are using is modified gaming software or modified simulator software. And any chemical used were simple chemicals mixed at the site." Clarkson added.

"Is this a foreign government-sponsored program?" Hunter asked.

"No sir, not directly. Most likely international. There is a Chinese team on U.S. soil looking for the same bunch of bastards. They probably had a similar catastrophe and followed the trail to us. Yesterday, when we checked the Purchase Orders at Miller, there were shipping parts to China, not the other way around. My guess is someone reassembled some device there and shot down one of their planes, and they are trying to find out who."

There was a silence that was expected as everyone weighed the gravity of what was being said.

"This is too big for your team alone. I am going to mobilize all the resistance to this disaster I can. In the meantime, your team has one primary job, and that is to slow these people down while we play catch up." Director Cunninham ordered.

"It was something from Agent Clarkson's question on why that particular plane. They may have gotten the idea from an unpublished novel by Sheldon. A blueprint to how to make this plan work. Bryan Sheldon was on flight 1317. He would have noticed his work when the plan went full swing." Anita explained.

"I got to bring in Homeland and the CIA. Chinese spies and Bosnian hitmen for crying out loud. This could start World War Three. And with that being said, how are you doing physically, Agent Tyler?" Director Cunnigham asked.

"Just a little hungry. I have been looking at this menu and having a hard time deciding what to try."

"I recommend the duck and noodles," Clarkson suggested.

Chapter 19

Anita was so happy to be back at the Spencer Hotel in Portland, even if she had been attacked in the elevator in this hotel. Anita was also delighted that Carolyn and saved the same rooms for the team. Anita took a hot shower and collapsed on the bed.

Carolyn's job now was to contact the local Claymore County police. The job of the local police was to locate, Morris Odel, the ghostwriter, and get eyes on him. When Odel was home for the evening, Clarkson and Anita would get a ride from the local police and visit Odel. The idea was to get as much information as they could without causing him to panic.

Anita did not mean to fall asleep, but she had. This time, Anita dreamed of sitting on the back porch of the family home holding a baby. The baby was the little girl who had lost her doll while waiting for flight 1317. In the dream, Anita's mother sat beside her as they rocked the child. A little boy threw a football backward and forth with a little girl. The little boy turned around and smiled at Anita and the child she rocked. The little boy was the little boy who had retrieved the lost doll for the small child. The little girl the boy was playing catch with turned and smiled at Anita. The little girl was her. Abruptly, Anita awakened.

ANITA DECIDED THAT sleep was not a good idea, so she went to the lobby to wait for her call by cell phone. This also was not the best choice as she ran into Justin, who had obviously had too much to drink.

"Look, before we dig a deeper hole for ourselves, would it do any good for me to start by apologizing to you for yelling at you the other day?" Anita asked.

"Apologize. Apologize for what? I thought standing in the middle of a muddy field screaming obscenities is just the way they communicate back in hog hollow."

"Look, it's not you. It's just that I can't seem to get those dead people off my mind, and I don't think I should."

"Look at you. You're an FBI throwaway, and you don't even have the brains to figure it out. They have you carrying the water for that old relic you call a boss. You keep doing the work, and every step of the way, the only reason the antiquated FBI is in front of the other agencies is your work. But wait until you make a mistake, there are going to turn on your pretty little ass like a pack of wild dogs." Justin sneered and moved closer toward Anita. "And if you stumble upon success by chance, who do you think will get the credit?"

"Agent Tyler, is this guy bothering you?" The question came for Hatcher, the swat team leader. Hatcher and his team had been given the night off by Clarkson and had heard the confrontation as they prepared to leave the hotel. The swat team was dressed in civilian clothing.

"Who the fuck are you?" Justin growled.

"I am FBI Swat team leader Hatcher. We have been assigned to protect Agents Clarkson and Tyler with our lives if need be. And before you say anything else stupid, I want to warn you my team takes their job extremely seriously."

Justin stood for a moment sizing up Hatcher and his team and knew he was outmatched. Justin started staggering off, then turned around and spoke. "A word to the wise team leader. You may want to watch your dick around that one. I hear if she gets mad; she will shoot it off."

With this, Justin went in search of more libation.

"Girl, you are going to have a hard time living that one down." Cook, the only female member of the team, said with a chuckle. Even in street clothes, Cook looked formidable. She had the build of a female ultimate fighter and a face that looked like she had endured her fair share of punches.

"We are going karaoke. Cook has the worst karaoke voice in the world. Do you want to join us?" Logan offered.

"No, I still have work to do with the boss. But if you guys hear of a place that has Texas Holdem one thousand to two thousand dollars buy-in, let me know."

Chapter 20

Odell lay naked in the darkness. He had just finished his second round of sex with Sasha. Odell had met Sasha this evening, and it seemed like the crowning touch to a personal celebration. Not that the death of the writer Bryan Sheldon was cause for celebration in itself, but Odell felt like a man who had spent his life digging in a mountain of rock, and now he had found the mother lode. A gold vein that promised to keep paying for the rest of his life. For years, Odell had worked in the shadows for the big publishing houses, cleaning up and finishing books for writers. They were too lazy, drunken, or just plain stupid to finish the projects they started and meet a deadline. And why had the publishing houses refused to give him contracts? He knew it was because he was not the look they wanted on the back of the books. Morris Odell was a large Blackman with a plain face. Odell had been a high school teacher in the roughest parts of East St. Louis, and he had a look that had backed down even some of the hardened young thugs.

Odell looked at Sasha's sleeping naked body. Sasha had made mad, passionate love to him with the greatest of skill and eroticism, all while separating it from fake emotional residual traces. She was the perfect stranger to have sex with. No guilt or remorse, just pure pleasure. Odell knew he suffered from some form of depression that stood in the way of most normal relationships with the opposite sex. Still, Sasha had been so accommodating, and she seemed to really listen when he spoke. He thought maybe when I get paid, I can get her to stick around for a while.

He further thought that now everyone would have to come through me. Someone was offering nine million dollars for the rights to the book, and with Sheldon dead, the rights were all his. Maybe there is some justice in this cold, cruel life, he thought.

"HE PICKED UP A GIRL at a hotel bar and drove home. The lights went out a couple of hours ago. They should both be pretty worn out by now, and it should make your arrest easy." The Moline County sheriff stated.

The sheriff's deputies had followed Odell from his home to the hotel bar and then back to the house.

"Who is the girl?" Anita asked.

"No idea. We got pictures, but no one from my squad recognized her. She is a cute little number, but she aint local."

Anita and Clarkson sat in the back of the police vehicle en route to Odell's home. Anita and Clarkson agreed they needed to speak to Odell and find out what he knew. Clarkson was becoming increasingly a fan of Anita's talent for reading the tells in people's mannerisms and facial clues.

ODELL WENT INTO THE bathroom and was taking a leak when there was a knock on the door.

"Police, Mr. Odell, we have some FBI officials that need to talk to you." The sheriff called out in an official voice.

Odell walked back into the room and saw Sasha standing by the bed. Sasha had put on Odell's shirt and had slipped back into her panties. She was now standing there with a gun in her hand. Odell could not pinpoint what was going on. He walked toward Sasha to try to calm her down when he noticed she was as calm as he had ever seen a person. Sasha fired twice into Odell's chest, then turned and ran toward the entry door. She emptied the clip into the door. Sasha then ran and jumped from the window in the bedroom and sprinted across the lawn.

Two deputies saw Sasha vault from the window and took off in foot pursuit, but Sasha was running so fast they were losing ground with every step. The two deputies looked winded as something shoved through the center of them. It was not something but someone. Anita ran past the deputies like they were running backward. Sasha slowed down for a fraction of a second to decide whether to run right or left, and Anita tackled her with a flying open-field tackle.

"Bullshit." Anita could hear one of the deputies yelled as he saw Anita wrestle Sasha and roll her over to handcuff her.

Sasha started yelling in a language none of the others understood.

"Get paramedics out here. Read her, her rights. Then lock her up and keep her isolated from anyone or anything. We need a Russin translator to re-read her rights to her." Clarkson commanded.

"Russian?" The sheriff said, walking up, putting his hands on his knees, and struggling for air. "Which department of the FBI did you two say you came from again?"

Chapter 21

While the police and FBI crime scene teams argued over jurisdiction and which facilities to store evidence, Anita accessed Morris Odell's computer. Odell lived alone and kept his passwords on sticky notes attached to his computer. She took a thumb drive and made a copy of his most recent manuscript, 'The Final Adjustment,' by checking the date the last data entries had been worked on.

Arriving back, Anita went to the hotel manager and had him open the business center at the Spencer Hotel, and she printed out a copy of the manuscript.

Anita now lay in bed in her hotel room reading the unpublished last works of Bryan Sheldon and Morris Odell. It was horrifying. Everything she had feared, and more was right in front of her. What was more frightening was that if this blueprint was followed, millions more would die. Country boundaries would be redrawn, and worldwide wealth would be redistributed. Her reading so compelled Anita that it took a while to notice someone knocking on her hotel room door. Mai Li, Anita thought the tortured woman who wanted to know her son had died for a good cause. Anita sprang to her feet and ran toward the door. Anita grabbed the half-finished bottle of Pettibone Brandy with one hand and flung open the door with the other. Instead of seeing Mai Li, Congresswoman Fletcher stood there, the woman who was Justin's boss and had mistaken her for Clarkson's daughter.

"Looks like you were expecting someone else." The Congresswoman snatched the bottle of brandy from Anita's hand and took a moment to eye her current state of dress. Anita was wearing only an old Seminole jersey she had received from one of her brothers and used as a nightgown.

Congresswoman Fletcher located a glass, poured some of the liquor, and then looked at it for a moment. "Well, maybe I misjudged you a second time. Here, I thought you were too simple to know a good thing when you see it, and I find you go for the good stuff."

"How can the FBI help you, ma'am." Anita noticed the Congresswoman had already been drinking and wanted the conversation to be as brief and non-confrontational as possible.

"My so aren't we fucking civil. But I heard there is another side to you that can be downright rude." The Congresswoman seated herself without invitation.

"So, your aid gets his feeling hurt by a little rejection, and he goes crying to mommy." Anita knew she had trouble controlling her sassy side but could not resist the open challenge.

"Listen, miss hot pants. I was in a meeting with the directors of the FBI, and they were arguing over who gets you after this shit gets cleared up. Our mutual friend, the General, was there, and he said you are still technically army property on loan to the FBI. He wants to induce you to reenlist, take a promotion, and use you in Military Intelligence."

"Let me take a wild guess. You came here to make me a better offer."

"Listen to me, you snot nose little hick. You can have any guy you want right now, but you will be surprised how fast that passes. A girl must know her worth upfront to prepare for the future."

"So, you are assuming my ass is for sale?" Anita taunted.

"Is it that big strapping Hatcher that you were waiting for to seal the deal, so to speak, when I showed up? There's no reason you can't have him, too. A girl in the right position with the right person backing them can have anything they want."

"Ma'am, that is just plain rude and inappropriate. I will ask you to leave and take the rest of the bottle with you. I have some reading to do."

Anita opened the door and waited for the Congresswoman to leave.

Chapter 22

"Sasha Abramov, aka Myra Kyrylenko, aka Valentina Zemtosova, aka Olga Tereshkova, aka a lot of other hard to pronounce fake ass names. You have been a very bad girl. You are a hired killer wanted in at least four countries. My name is Agent Stockton, and as of this minute, your pretty little ass belongs to me." Agent Stockton started the interrogation as a form of intra-governmental territorial pissing contest. Sasha had been brought to an interrogation room and chained to a steel table. Anita and Clarkson sat eyeing Sasha, and Sasha sat staring unmoved by Stockton. Anita noticed that Sasha now did not look the same as the wild woman fighting to get away only hours before. Sasha looked like she had been scrubbed within an inch of her life. Sasha wore a glow-in-the-dark orange jumpsuit that was two sizes too large for her and made her look like an angry child.

Without moving her head, Sasha rolled her large green eyes to Clarkson. "You had me segregated from the rest of the population; why?"

"I am Senior Agent Clarkson of the FBI. This is Agent Tyler. I had you segregated because it has been my experience that when a hit fails, they send someone to tie up loose ends."

"So, as a man, you are protecting me?" Sashas harsh lower class Russian accent bite into the air.

"Call it a professional courtesy on my part. I am asking nothing in return."

Much of the sarcasm on Sasha's face faded for an instant.

"Now that we are all good friends let's get back to business. I say we put your hot little ass on the first plane back to Russia, where they believe in capital punishment in the express lane. Hell, you probably won't make it out of the Moscow airport before they put a bullet in your skank ass. Unless you want to tell me something about jets falling out of the sky." Stockton commanded.

"It was not my wish to kill him." Sasha looked now at Anita. Anita saw the connection that Sasha was trying to make with her.

"So, let's see, you are a hired killer who just can't get enough of that Mandingo dick."

"Stop talking," Anita yelled, shocked by the force in her own voice as she commanded Stockton to stop.

Stockton looked insulted. "Look, let's not fall for this. I'm sorry, I just had to do it shit. This whore had laid a path of corpses across Europe and into China. Now she brings her sorry ass...."

"Agent Stockton, can we speak outside for a moment?" It was more a statement from Clarkson than a question, and Clarkson noticed the connection Sasha seemed to be building with Anita.

"THIS IS AN FBI TRICK," Sasha stated after Stockton and Clarkson had left the room.

"I have only been with the FBI for less than a week. They haven't taught me any tricks yet. My boss is like my coach or trainer and doesn't want me picking up bad habits." Anita smiled a little and found it relieved her a bit. She was getting upset with Stockton more than Sasha.

"I did not want to kill Morris. He was a good man. He was lonely." Sasha seemed surprised as her revelation came forth."

"I know," Anita answered. "But Morris Odell is not dead. He is in critical condition, but he is fighting to stay alive."

An unmistakable wave of relief came over Sasha's face for a split second, and then quickly, she reverted to the hardened criminal. "You are fast. You should be in the Olympics."

"My sister is a lot faster, and she is trying out for the Olympics."

"Aren't you supposed to be questioning me?"

"Why. I know you shoot him because you thought we were coming to take you back to Russia."

Sasha softens for a moment. "I like a man who can build things with his hands, but I love a man who can build things with his mind. I could have made him happy as his girlfriend or his wife. I overheard him talking to someone arguing over his percent of a nine-million-dollar deal on his cell phone."

The women sat momentarily, watching the door where Stockton and Clarkson were unclear on how to proceed. Anita could read many stories on Sasha, but she felt like she might be invading the woman's privacy in some ways.

"They made an agreement. Instead of the fifty-fifty Morris wanted, they agreed on forty, and Morris gets equal credit on the book cover and for the movie deal. Now I have spilled my guts you tell me how is Morris?"

"We are hoping he makes it. We don't think he was involved, but he may have information we need to prosecute others later."

"I got so tired of the poverty, the beating, and the rape that I made myself strong. Until you knocked on that door, the images faded. They all rushed back. He deserves a better woman than me. Will you tell him that for me?"

ANITA FOUND CLARKSON in a breakroom at the federal facility. Clarkson was talking to his wife, and Anita took the phone to update Mrs. Clarkson on Agent Clarkson's latest eating and fashion changes. For the first time, Anita felt conflicted speaking with Mrs. Clarkson.

Here was a woman who had suffered the loss of a daughter and was dying from cancer. She had grown tired of seeing her husband sit at her bedside, watching her wither away, and had sent him back to work. But still, Anita felt a kinship with Mai Li as well, a woman left with the most incredible reminders of the man she loved but could not keep. Anita knew poker cleared her head, but she was afraid to try to find a table to play at after being attacked on the elevator at the Spencer Hotel; she did not want to carry danger around with her, forcing it on innocent people. This as Melony's problem she thought not hers, she is a Tyler not Clarkson's daughter. Why should she care so much that both Mrs. Clarkson and Mai Li receive their rightful allotment of Agent Clarkson's comfort for their losses?

ERIC AND CAROLYN MET Anita and Clarkson in the lobby of the Spencer upon their arrival. Eric and Carolyn stood in the middle of a large amount of luggage.

"You guys look tired. I guess you can rest on the plane."

"What plane?" Anita asked.

"There will be an IRS raid on Planet Publishing, the publishing house that has worked with Sheldon. Payments for parts and materials were traced from the Miller manufacturing to the Publishing company. There should be no connection from a manufacturing company to a Publishing house, but there they are. They are partially responsible for funding this disaster. They want us there when they serve the warrant." Eric explained.

"Who packed for me?" Anita asked.

"Eric insisted," Carolyn answered.

Anita gave Eric a suspicious look.

"Carolyn is color blind, or did you not notice how much like a clown you looked the last time she helped you with clothes."

"Little dude, I don't know whether to hug you for saving me or whack you upside the head for invading my privacy."

"Figure it out on the plane. New York is a long way away." Clarkson decided.

Chapter 23

On the plane, Anita sat next to Clarkson, watching him rest. "Thank you." She spoke.

"For what?"

"For letting me speak to Sasha alone."

"Even a dinosaur like me could see her tighten up at Stockton's every word."

Anita went over what she had learned from Sasha.

Clarkson sat with his eyes closed. "What did the Congresswoman want?"

"So, you are having me watched?" Anita snapped.

"Yes, I have been having someone watch the three of you since you got on the elevator with a Bosnian kill team and started getting in the elevator with carloads of Chinese spies."

"Fair enough. She wanted to offer me a job."

"Doing what?"

"I think she thinks I would be a good personal inside FBI mole."

"So, did you take the job?"

Anita looked at him and smiled. "Of course not. She says who her people sleep with, and that I find repulsive."

Clarkson adjusted in his seat as if he was going to get some sleep. "One other question."

"Yes." Anita braced herself for the worst.

"Is your father still doing his pathetic Mick Jagger karaoke impersonations."

Anita laughed. "If you knew how much I love my folks, you would not be so quick to make fun, Sir. I miss them and have not been in touch with them since this thing started. This being work for national security and all. But I did hear that my brother Lavon is marrying Lynn Tyler."

"So, your brother is marrying one of your sisters?"

"No sir, that would be stupid. Lynn's last name is something else, but my father made her a Tyler temporarily because Kim, one of my sisters, broke her leg, and we needed a replacement Tyler girl for the charity games; otherwise, we would have had to forfeit the tug of war."

"Please keep talking, Tyler. You are putting me to sleep, and I need the rest."

Clarkson rested, and Anita did as well.

Chapter 24

The trip had been hard so far. There was a stop in Dallas to change planes. Anita was unsure how flying in the wrong direction was the fastest route but did not ask. Anita found that she had to be sure Eric paid attention to when they were supposed to board in that he would start reading or looking things up on his computer and totally black out everyone.

Carolyn kept finding men to talk to. At one point, Anita thought she had lost Carolyn until she saw in the airport what looked like a circle of giant redwood trees with shiny shoes. It was Carolyn in the middle of a circle of Army rangers about to give the punchline for a dirty joke. Anita spirited Carolyn off, much to the dismay of the Rangers.

The Crompton Excelsior of New York and the Spencer Hotel of Portland, Oregon, were both hotels, but that is where the similarities ended. The Spencer was a large hotel with many rooms set up to accommodate business interactions. The Crompton was a massive structure. The Crompton had four main wings that were built all to themselves, connected by walkways or sky bridges. The Crompton had twenty-eight floors and a countless number of elevators, corridors, and staff.

When the team reached the check-in desk, a small Hispanic woman began giving out room assignments. The rooms for the four were not only on different floors but in different wings of the hotel.

This meant that, for all practical purposes, they were staying in separate buildings.

"So much for my plan to keep you all safe," Clarkson grumbled, staring at the woman behind the hotel counter.

"This is like a three-dimensional treasure map." Carolyn joked, and she looked at maps showing how to locate the different rooms.

"Everybody sleeps with your doors locked and your Glocks cocked. If you shoot a maid or two by accident, let me know. I will be happy to help you with the paperwork." Clarkson grumbled and popped a piece of the nicotine gum in his mouth.

Anita turned around at a noise and was distracted by a banner in the hotel displaying a poker tournament.

"And no poker for you until we close this mess. There is a meeting tonight, and I need you, or top of your FBI tell game, Agent Tyler." Clarkson insisted.

Chapter 25

Anita walked past the mirror in the hotel room, preparing for the meeting. She was startled by the woman she saw staring back at her. Only days ago, Anita had prayed to God, trying to strike a bargain. She questioned that he had chosen the correct warrior to avenge the death of those people from Flight 1317. But when she looked at the woman in the mirror, she could see the changes in herself. Maybe God was making her who she would need to be to complete this mission. Or perhaps she was becoming Melody to appease the wishes of a man whose life descended through the hourglass of time as the lives of all men do.

SINCE ANITA HAD NO experience with IRS raids, she found the experience a significant learning opportunity. Anita was surprised at how polite and professional the IRS agents were. They asked questions and waited for complete answers before continuing. When the IRS agents asked for documents or records, they escorted whoever was retrieving or looking up the records and supervised the handling. They collected huge amounts of files.

Anita noticed Eric doing his best to hide that he was motion-sick again. The flight to New York was long, with a layover that seemed to take forever. Anita wrestled with asking Carolyn to please stop trying to force Eric to be jealous long enough for the poor soul to recuperate but was afraid the request would have the reverse effect.

"MISS COOPER, I WOULD like for you to meet Senior FBI Agent Clarkson and Agent Anita Tyler." Carolyn introduced a frail woman sitting, shaking, and sweating in a chair in the company's accounts receivable department. The physical layout of Planet Publishing was like that of many companies that deal in intellectual property. There was plush carpeting and cubicles for the employees who scurried about their jobs like worker bees.

"Miss Cooper was in the process of lying to me about a matter of national security, and I think you guys might get a kick out hearing what she has to say before I book her a room in the harshest woman's prison I can find," Carolyn stated in a cold tone.

"Have you read Miss Cooper her rights yet?" Clarkson asked.

"She waived them for the time being. She says this is all a misunderstanding, and if we arrest her, her career is over." Carolyn answered and looked at Anita. Anita knew that was why Carolyn wanted her in the room. Carolyn knew Miss Cooper was lying but had to see where the lie began and ended.

"Miss Cooper, why don't you tell me what the misunderstanding is? Maybe I can explain it to Carolyn and my boss." Anita requested.

"It was a gift. All these people sign contracts for advances that are more than I paid for my house. Now someone throws a little money my way, and the earth starts shaking." Miss Cooper stated in a rattled voice. Her eyes darted about as if trying to determine who it was the was the most important for her to convince.

"How much?" Anita asked.

"The way it works is that money is kept in large blocks because it earns higher interest rates. Two million was allocated for Sheldon's book. Then, the two million went back to the company account. That means someone bought the manuscript from under Planets Publishing's nose. And Miss Cooper made that happen by not paying Sheldon or Odell." Carolyn stated.

"Making their contract claims void and letting them sell to someone else," Clarkson added.

"How much god damn it?" Anita stated sharply. She was not happy that Miss Cooper did not answer her question.

"Two hundred fifty thousand dollars." Miss Cooper's answer fell on the group and caused a momentary silence.

"Read this bitch her rights and cuff her," Anita commanded in an angrier voice than anyone in the room had heard come from her before. "You sold your soul for pieces of silver and gold and allowed those babies to be burned to death and dropped from the sky."

"Tell the IRS she is ours. After we finish with her, she goes to Homeland, and if there is any meat left on the carcass after we finish, she is all theirs." Clarkson decided.

"We have a much larger problem, Boss." Anita knew Clarkson had also read the manuscript and knew where the greater problem lay.

"Carolyn, find Eric, and as soon as he stops puking in guts out, track down that agent for Sheldon and Odell. Contact TSA and any locals in her area. No way she slips out of the country." Clarkson commanded.

Chapter 26

The confusion at the counter where the name tags were being handed out made the confusion at the hotel check-in counter pale in comparison.

"Look, meathead, my name is Carolyn Lang. The name tag says, Carol Lee Chang. Do I look Chinese to you?"

"Ma'am, we don't discriminate here at the hotel." A man in an army uniform who looked too young to be a soldier answered.

Anita thought it was funny until they handed her a name tag. It read Andrew Tyler-Department of Justice.

"I'm not with the DOJ Anita answered," Anita informed the lad.

"Doesn't the FBI report to the DOJ?"

"And the fact that I am a girl and not a boy should matter even if we are in New York." Anita sharply responded.

"I must remind you to always keep your name tags on during the session. The Marines have security, and when they are told they can throw someone out of a meeting if they take the name tag off, and I hear they take that command literally." The young lad gave Anita a final last word look.

The conference room was packed with people from various agencies discussing the developments related to flight 1317 and the investigation's progress. Anita had not located Clarkson, but she knew he was in the room somewhere.

"Hey Tyler, the boss wants to know if you are hiding from her."

Anita turned around to see a puggy man in a suit two sizes too small. Not only was Anita sure she did not know the man, but she also could tell he wasn't talking to her. The puggy man was calling someone behind her. Anita turned abruptly and collided with a muscular man with a boyish face. The man she ran into had sandy hair and a genuine grin, and he wore a dark three-piece suit. The most noticeable thing about the man was that his name tag read Anita Tyler FBI.

"Oh, thank goodness." Anita proclaimed.

"I don't think anybody that has run me over has ever given that response." The man had a southern accent but was not in the middle of Mississippi like Anita's. It was smoother.

"South Carolina." Anita guessed.

"For generations. And you, Mississippi."

The man had caught Anita to keep her from toppling over when the two collided but had not noticed they had not released each other. Embarrassed, Anita pulled back. "You have my name tag."

"And I see you have mine."

They began switching name tags, and someone called out. "Hey, Drew, I would be careful with that one." Anita looked over her shoulder, and it was Justin.

"Oh, you know Justin." Great disappointment registered in Andrew's voice.

"No, not like that. He is one of many jerks who doesn't like to take no for an answer."

Andrew and Anita noticed he had stepped back when he asked if she knew Justin. "I'm sorry if I seem judgmental. I guess that lifestyle is suited for some." Andrews's eyes fell as he explained, showing he was genuinely concerned about how Anita perceived him.

Anita located Clarkson. The meeting room was set up similarly to a courtroom, with two stands for speakers and microphones. The setup was clearly to give the speaker information for the record.

"I hope we run into each other again sometime, Agent Tyler," Andrew called out as Anita skirted away. She knew he was still watching her, and it made her feel good.

"Making new friend, Agent Tyler?" Clarkson asked when Anita joined him at their assigned station.

Anita looked at Clarkson and lowered his voice so only he could hear. "He seems nice. Do you know him?"

"Not really." Clarkson gave a smug grin. "Maybe after you, too, stop having eyeball sex, you can introduce yourself to him."

"Do you think..." Anita began, then stopped speaking and started looking at the papers in front of her.

"Agent Tyler. Anita Tyler, I would trust your instincts over even my own at this point. If my daughter had half your talent for knowing when something was wrong, she would still be alive today. She trusted someone from another agency, and they sold her out. They may or may not have known it would be a death sentence for her, but all the same, she is dead."

Anita did not know how to respond. She was now close enough for Clarkson to reveal more about himself. But there was a great deal of pain in his voice. Anita now knew she could not vilify him for his past indiscretion. Anita could see he was more than a friend of her father, and he was more than a teacher or coach. Anita now knew Waldren Clarkson was a man, born of sinew and bone and subject to the same questionable choices as any other human.

THE MEETING PROCEEDED much as Anita thought it would. Several speeches from government department heads wanted a chance to make political speeches. After a time, Clarkson was called to the podium. Clarkson took Anita by the arm and brought her with him. Anita was nervous; like many people, she had not spoken before an audience since high school. But as apprehensive as she was, she felt this was her chance to speak out about the loss on flight 1317.

"Based on the information we have at this time, there is a group of individuals that are positioning themselves to destroy the government as we know it today." You could hear a pin drop after Clarkson's opening statement. "Make no mistake, we are going after them with every resource the United States Government can muster. But that may not be enough."

"Excuse me for asking, but if this is so grievous, why do you have an untrained agent working beside you? No offense to the female gender but are there not men with more experience and more qualified to watch your back." The interruption came from Justin.

Clarkson stared for a moment, then reached into his pocket and pulled out a piece of the nicotine gum. "Sorry for the delay; I have been quitting smoking, and sometimes I need a piece of nicotine gum." Now, Anita was a little nervous, not knowing what her boss's next words would be. "Two highly trained assassins got on an elevator with my new partner a couple of days ago. And before you ask, she is just fine. However, the two assholes who attacked her are in critical condition fighting for their lives and evaluating their choice of rookies to assault. As I said, Agent Tyler is fine, as proven by the next day. She then ran down on foot by an international professional assassin wanted in four counties and cuffed her." Clarkson stopped and looked at Justin for a moment. "With this type of commitment to getting the job done, I can think of no better person, man, woman, or anything in between, to watch my back, sir."

A group of female agents stood in the back, and they began applauding. Soon, the entire room joined in congratulating Anita. Anita looked around for Andrew, but he seemed to have left the room. She was disheartened. It was starting to seem like the story of her life. No sooner than she met a nice guy, he was gone, or her responsibilities took her away.

"Agent Tyler, what do you have to say?" The chairman asked as the cheers died down.

"Mr. Chairperson, the people that are a part of this crime are attempting to put in place a World War 2 do-over," Anita informed.

"What is their political affiliation?" Someone quickly asked.

"We don't think they have one. It is all about redistributing wealth. First, think about all the companies that got wealthy because of the ramp-up in need caused by World War 2. And now, think about all the companies and industries that went bankrupt during those times. If you knew a great catastrophe was on the horizon, you could prepare to profiteer." Clarkson explained.

"How can someone be planning such a horrible thing?" Someone asked.

Clarkson looked at Anita, and she fielded the question. "Most people think that if there is a World War 3, it will be nuclear. But this is not about World War 3. It is about a World War 2 do-over. By shipping parts to countries for conventional weapons and having them reassembled, these bad people can cause conventional fighting all over the globe. The battles seem unrelated, but all are designed to serve a central purpose."

"This sounds too farfetched." Someone stated from the crowd.

"Take their word for it. The Chinese had a jet loaded with diplomats shot down, and they thought it was the US." A voice cooperated from a dark corner of the room.

"And how do you know this?" The chairman asked.

"Because I am with the CIA, Sir, it's my job to know these things." The man stepped forward, and the light revealed his face; it was Agent Stockton. "The weapons they have been able to construct so far are not designed to last for an extended period. They don't have to, the plan is to start conventional conflicts throughout the world followed by even more dangerous finger pointing."

Chapter 27

A nita sat in the bed of her hotel room of the Crompton, staring at the picture of the small children who were exchanging kindness just before flight 1317. Anita still felt energized from the meeting. People had recognized her efforts. Not only people recognized her but Agent Clarkson, a man cut from the same cloth as her father.

Anita had stopped by Eric's room in the maze of humongous hotel rooms and had brought him some over-the-counter medicine she had located, along with a scolding for trying to be the big man and suffer through. Anita also lectured Eric on not letting Carolyn's flirtatious ways cause him grief. Her deliberate attempts to make him jealous further prove that even though they worked together excellently as a team, they were not compatible as a couple.

There was a slight knock on the hotel room door. Anita collected her Glock 19 before proceeding to check who was there.

"I came bearing gifts." Mai Li announced when Anita discovered it was her.

Anita gave Mai Li a big hug and ushered her into the room.

"I could not find my oblong tea, so I brought some Pettibone Brandy instead. Let us see if you can use a corkscrew opener for its true intended purposes." Mai Li joked, holding up a large bottle of brandy with one hand and a large package of fig cookies with the other. Mai had done a poor imitation of Anita's country accent.

The women sat and socialized momentarily, and then Anita realized Mai Li was staring into her drink.

"John was a perfect child. I know most parents feel that way about their children. But he was. He never cried as a child. He only watched me. Growing up, knowing how I was doing seemed so important to him. My father is a General, and he never recognized John. So, none of my family had the fortitude to defy the General, and John instinctively knew it was me and him against the world. Every day, I fought not to tell him Waldren was his father. But I knew the mess that would cause."

Anita now knew why Mai Li coming back to visit her was so important. It was so both could share grief in the loosing of the life of children. To Anita's own astonishment, she realized she was in some ways grieving for two small children she had never met. And Mai Li was grieving for the loss of her son.

"Agent Tyler."

"Please call me Anita. I don't work for you or with you. I want to believe we are two friends."

"Anita, I have been reading about this game of poker, and I understand that lying is allowed, as is deception of other forms."

"Yes, it is a part of the game."

"So, if you are good at this game, that means you know how to lie or at the least to be less than straightforward when it is called for."

Anita had yet to learn where Mai Li was going.

"That will depend on who you think I should lie to."

"Anita, my friend, I have a piece of intelligence that I cannot use for reasons that may become evident to you. But you can use it. About a year ago, I was assigned to a case where a mass grave with about fifty of my fellow countrymen had been buried. My investigation revealed that the worker had been used to assemble one of the death machines. When the workers are no longer of use, they are executed."

"I don't know if I packed for a trip out of the country."

"A similar project is currently in process in the United States, and no one in your government seems to have a clue."

Anita took another big swallow from her Pettibone Brandy, trying to wash down the reality of what was being said. "You want me and my team to save those people's lives and stop whatever machine they are building. But I cannot be specific about how I got the information."

"Exactly. Dear Anita, many in my government believe that the war machine that killed those Chinese diplomats was either directed or sold by the US, and I would love for the West to suffer the same loss. Don't you see my baby's death proves the opposite? Please, I ask you as a friend, don't let my baby have died in vain."

Mai Li sat scribbling information on a hotel notepad that Anita would need.

"You still love him, don't you?"

Without turning around or looking up, Mai Li knew it was Waldren Clarkson, whom Anita had asked about. "With all my heart. And I am so glad you have been choosing his ties." Mai Li chuckled slightly.

"I think Carolyn has been doing it, and she is a good person, but she is color blind and fashion coordination challenged. And coming from a girl straight off a Mississippi farm town, that is saying a lot."

The women worked for a while, and Mai Li made sure Anita understood the information. Anita listened closely and asked few questions but still wanted to know how Mai Li would always know where Clarkson would be.

Chapter 28

Anita didn't need to discuss where she had obtained the information on the puzzle assembly operations on US soil. Clarkson knew but chose not to discuss it. Instead, Clarkson started putting together the plan for the raid on the assembly operation. The assembly operation was being done in a small rural area outside of Portland, Oregon.

Eric reported that Rachel Galloway, the literary agent for Sheldon and Odell, had been arrested. Rachel was attempting to board a flight to Switzerland. But the TSA handed her over to federal agents and, after processing, would be sent to the FBI facility in Portland to await questioning.

The FBI operates 56 of its swat teams in various levels across the US, but for this operation, Clarkson chose to request the aid of the United States Army. Since whoever or whatever was on the ground where they were going could shoot down aircraft, Clarkson wanted aerial surveillance from a distance where the observers were out of range or undetected by whoever was on the ground. Clarkson was also worried that if someone was assembling robotic automated Gatling guns as they had on his previous raid, even the best swat team may not be prepared to handle the results.

The General had arranged two REO M35 trucks with two twenty-person assault teams and two helicopters to aid in the raid.

"Scorekeeper to the Coach, we count over fifty warm bodies in three manmade structures on the property. Awaiting your green light."

The Army Captain in charge of the primary assault informed Clarkson. Anita had chosen Clarkson's handle for the operation.

"Operations a go. All warrants are in hand. Move." Clarkson commanded, and the two trucks rolled out from a point near the fire road where the occupant of the assembly area could not spot them. Two groups of soldiers with automatic weapons converged on the area just, and the two helicopters landed in the front of the structures. The assault was with precision, and as people started attempting to run, they were rounded up. The workers were average people, some computer workers and some skilled at assembly. They needed to figure out how the instruments they were constructing would be used.

The first building was the computer hub and data center for the operation. Eric went to work securing the information that would be needed to determine the progress the people trying to topple governments had made.

The second building was made to look like a barn but was the assembly point for huge items that were nowhere to be found. The third building was an unmanned attack drone. The drone looked like a US attack drone but had no markings.

"Jesus Christ." The captain said. "Where the hell did this monster come from."

A soldier ran into the hangar as Anita, Clarkson, and the Captain were examining the drone. "We got runners. Two vehicles were headed here, but they saw our party and then turned around. They are hightailing it up the fire road. We might lose them if they make it to the main highway."

"Permission to pursue." The captain asked Clarkson.

"Permission granted; Agent Tyler is going with you. She has tactical command." Clarkson confirmed.

Clarkson looked at Anita as though he needed to say something to her, and he did only without words.

"I know, coach. I read the manuscript, and I have an idea with protocols these guys are working off if they stick to the plot from the book."

Chapter 29

It took no time for the helicopters to locate the vehicles driving as fast as they could down the dirt road and spewing rock and gravel everywhere. Anita was in helicopter two when helicopter one flew up and hovered in front of the lead vehicle. The led vehicle was a large jeep with something attached to the back under a cover. The second vehicle was a conversion van and did not look like it should be off-road.

"This is the US Army. We are assisting the FBI in serving a warrant. Please stop your vehicle at once." One of the soldiers from helicopter one called out over a speaker.

Both vehicles stopped. Too easy, Anita thought, just as a man jumped out of the jeep with an AK47 and began shooting at helicopter one. Helicopter two had an open door with a machine gun mounted. "Permission to engage Tactical Leader."

"Pilot, swing this crate around; Gunner shoot to kill." It took less than a second for Anita to give the command, and the man with the AK47 was shredded by the gunner in Helicopter Two.

Helicopter one had taken gunfire and was trailing smoke and was forced to land. Just then, the sliding door to the conversion van opened, and an automated ramp began coming out. At first glance, Anita knew it was the same type of automatic machine gun that had fired on the FBI team only days before. Anita knew when the gun had fully extended, and the infrared sights were activated on the automated machine gun. The game was over for her and her crew.

"Pilot, swing around and give the gunner a clear line of fire." Anita's father had been a police chief before becoming a novelist. All the Tyler children knew firearms and how they were best used. "Gunner, on your first available opportunity, I want you to destroy the motherfucker, and I don't give a shit who is in the passenger seat."

"Copy that, Tactical Leader, and by the way, I think I am in love." The gunner replied as he released a volley of gunfire that set the van into full blaze. A ragged man with a beard ran from the blaze of the van and then fell to the ground.

AS ANITA, THE PILOT, and the Gunner made it to the driver of the conversion van, it was clear he was dead.

"Quarterback, this is Little Dude; come in."

Anita heard the walkie-talkie call her. "What you got for me, Little Dude? We are a little busy?"

"That done fired itself up and took off, and nobody could do anything to stop it. The coach says he thinks it is following the protocol from the manuscript. Anita, I did not read it, but I think you are in danger."

"Roll him over and pull his pants down." Anita dropped the walkie-talkie and yelled at the gunner.

"What?" The Pilot and Gunner said in unison.

Anita dropped to her knees and began pulling the man's pants down. She spread the butt cheeks of the dead man. There was a square patch showing something had been implanted beneath the skin.

"What the fuck is that." The pilot asked.

"He has a chip under his skin like the chip on a dog. This is a protocol for covering evidence. When this guy's heart stopped beating, the drone set itself to destroy the evidence."

"Give us the brief version of what is about to happen." The gunner requested.

"The drone is going to fire on this site to destroy the body and the vehicles. I will make a pass and kill anything with a warm body mass that may be human on the ground." The pilot looked at the injured team from helicopter one in the distance. "Then it will crash itself into the computer hub and destroy that evidence."

"Look, tactical, you know what it means someone has to do." The pilot looked at helicopter two.

"The drone is too fast and too well armed for the helicopter to have a one-on-one gunfight with." Anita assessed.

"Only if both gunfighters are playing to win."

Anita knew in an instant what he was proposing, and he only needed her permission to complete his plan.

"Quick, give me your dog tags." Anita kissed the pilot on the cheek as he handed over his tags. "Permission granted."

Anita turned to the gunner. "We have to try to get everyone to the ditch and hope the done has to take a second pass to line up to shoot."

The pilot ran back to helicopter two and was off in an instant. The gunner and Anita ran as fast as they could to reach the wounded crew from helicopter one. Anita and her survivors had just made it to the ditch when a huge explosion and a flash of light followed a swoosh. The drone had the capability to shoot both the jeep and the conversion van with rockets on a single pass, but just she had hoped it had to make a second pass to machine gun the survivors on the ground. As the drone made it out of its arch to drop into shooting position, Anita and the other helicopter survivors saw helicopter two. Helicopter two made a figure-eight loop and nose-dived into the drone's path. A shock wave followed a large explosion, and fragments pelted the surviving onlookers, but they did not look away or duck for cover. They all stood there accepting the pelting of dirt and small rocks from the blast. No one said anything. They all knew the sacrifice the pilot had made that they might live another day. Anita stood for a moment, staring down at the dog tags. Her hand was bleeding from squeezing the tags, but she did not care.

"Look over there." A battered, bloody soldier from helicopter one prodded.

Anita saw the burning pile of rubble that once was a jeep with something strapped on the back beneath a cover. Anita was confused as to why this was significant.

"That is your surface-to-air killer, Team Leader. Looks like you set them back a step or two."

Chapter 30

"Do you think you made a mistake?" Clarkson asked Anita. Anita had said little during the cleanup and information gathering after the raid. The team was now flying back to the FBI office in Portland to question Rachel Galloway.

"No," Anita answered, still looking out the window of the plane.

"Well, is there anything you could have done differently?"

"No."

"Did you bring home as many of the people you were responsible for as possible?"

"Yes, Sir."

"Agent Tyler, I have never been prouder of an agent as when you, without hesitation, made the same exact moves I would have made had I been there. Minus the kiss on the cheek. I did hear about that."

Anita smiled a little. She lightly touched her lips, remembering the kiss to send off the pilot. It was not a kiss born of romance or tenderness or of love. It was a kiss that said good-bye for what we as humans consider forever. May we perhaps meet again in the everlasting circle of infinity. "Coach, the army is going to do its standard notification of death to the family of Raymond Hargrove, the pilot who sacrificed his life."

"Yes, that's about right."

"I want your permission to write them a handwritten letter. I won't put any details of the operation, just that he decided to save the lives of his team members without hesitation when he knew there was no

100

other way." The request came out as less of a plea and more of a firm negotiation. This was part of the new Anita she was becoming, and she knew there would be no stopping even if she wanted to.

"Agent Tyler, Anita, if you have been wondering why you are with us, that is exactly why. To do those things I cannot or will not do myself. Permission granted. And by the way, whatever you gave Eric seems to be working a good job on that, too."

WHEN RACHEL GALLOWAY was brought into interrogation, not unlike Sasha, Rachel had been scrubbed, scraped, and prodded to the degree that not only dirt and germs but a layer of her dignity had been removed as well. Also, unlike Sasha, since Clarkson and Anita had been busy elsewhere when Rachel was arrested, no one had insisted that Rachel be kept isolated. Rachel was having much trouble adjusting to being locked up that first-time prisoners experienced, as evidenced by her black eye and split lip. Rachel sat beside her new lawyer, Mr. Atwater, an abundantly serious-looking middle-aged man with significant hair loss.

"Agents, what exactly can you do to help my client?" Atwater volleyed as soon as Clarkson and Anita entered the room.

"Well, I can do my best to resist the urge to spit on her and call her nasty names," Anita answered.

"What my junior associate is trying to say is that we were originally being brought here to interrogate your client and perhaps see if there is something we could offer for her cooperation." Clarkson attempted to clear up.

Rachel sat there with a deer trapped in the headlights look.

"What changed?" Atwater asked, confused.

"Well, you know how you changed the companies sponsoring the book, The Final Adjustment? Well, the federal prosecutors made a change to the game as well. They went to Ms. Cooper, one of your co-conspirators' and questioned her first." Anita began.

"The prosecutor's office is modifying charges even as we speak," Clarkson added.

It would help if you had given her a more significant cut of the blood money. Anita suggested.

"What if my client can name names? And give you companies that are involved?" Atwater suggested.

"She will name names. You see, I am a good poker player, and the reason my boss wanted me here in the room with you is that I can spot a tell better than most." Anita began.

"So, parlor tricks aside, you still need evidence to convict," Atwater stated in a smug voice. Something in his tone did not sit quite well with Rachel, he was playing Anita's game, and now it was more apparent to Rachel.

"So, Counselor, we have the records from Miller Manufacturing and the copies of the record from Planet Publishing; we will be rounding up anyone involved in this major conspiracy to overthrow the government," Clarkson explained.

"If by chance we miss anybody, we will then take anything her pathetic ass has to offer. Right now, the plan is to flush her with the rest of the truds." Anita commented. "You see, you are right. The stuff said about lethal injection was all to get a response out of you, and it worked like a charm. The truth is I want you to live a long and painful life. And by the black eye and busted lip, I think the benefits of your new housing arrangement are starting to pay off. But of course, the women where you are headed are twice as hostile to baby killers."

"Oh God, make her stop. How could she be so hostile? It was only business." Rachel finally broke and cried out.

Anita reached into her pocket and took a picture of the two children in the Clearmont Airport exchanging kindness. "This is Fatima Patel. She was eighteen months old; the boy was Colton

Hawkins the third. You killed them with your unchecked greed and planning. Then you planned to celebrate by skying through a non-extradition country. Then you say well, that is just business." Anita adjusted and moved closer to Rachel as if they were the only ones in the room. "You transferred over a million dollars to your mother's bank account to hide funds. At this moment, a different team of FBI agents, along with IRS agents, are arresting your eighty-two-year-old mother from her senior living facility. Looks like she will be spending her golden years in a dungeon with a bunch of thug-ass women with parental issues."

"Is she insane?" Atwater asked Clarkson.

"Yes, but we still like seeing her carry the badge," Clarkson answered.

Chapter 31

"It doesn't seem fair. When I get used to having another hot chick around, we lose you." Carolyn stated. The FBI team had had a healthy morning breakfast, and all took turns speaking to Mrs. Clarkson over the phone.

"She isn't going for good. She has been accepted into the FBI academy's next class. With so many agencies and their underlings working on this case, no one will contest whether or not she is an official agent. We need to be sure she is official." Eric explained to the group.

"You do know you are going in on day one knowing more than any of the recruits will know when they graduate?" Carolyn asked.

"My first stop is to Shepherds Pass, Missouri. My brother is getting married. I am taking Eric with me. My younger sister Noreen needs an escort." Anita explained.

"Well, Agent Tyler, if you have a bunch of brothers, why are you not introducing me to them?" Carolyn asked.

"Because I would rather not have you screwing your way through the men in my family, thank you."

"I would be offended if that did not sound so sexy."

"Agent Tyler read the team your letter to the downed pilot," Clarkson instructed.

Dear Mr. and Mrs. Hardgrove'

By the time you receive this letter, you have most likely been informed of the death of your son Raymond. Please allow me to say first that I feel for your loss. Secondly, please allow me to state that I feel hurt and pain by the demise of your son myself.

I know that due to military protocol, specific details on your son's death are classified.

I knew your son for less than a full day. You are most likely wondering why someone who knew Raymond for less than a day felt compelled to write a personal letter. My answer is this: though not at liberty to give the details, your son assessed the dangers to his team and knew there was only one viable option to save their lives. Your son, not by order or selection but by his own choice, voluntarily saved the lives of his entire team. He did so by forfeiting his own life.

You should feel proud of how you brought your son up, even if it is little solace for his loss.

Raymond will not be coming home, but all the other members of his team will be able to return to their families because of his bravery.

Through selfless bravery, Raymond saved not only the lives of his teammates but my life as well. I hope to honor Raymond's memory by making wise choices and selflessly helping others as he did.

Respectfully submitted,

Anita

P.S. Due to the nature of my work, I have intentionally omitted my last name and my affiliation with the United States Government.

AFTER HER RECITATION, Anita stared down at the paper, wondering if it was what she wanted to say.

"Perfect. Now, we have a long way to go and a lot of bad people to arrest, so we need to get you back here as soon as possible." Clarkson stated.

Chapter 32

Agent Clarkson began packing for his flight home in the morning. There was a knock on his hotel room door. When he opened the door, the last person he thought would come to visit him was standing there. It was Mai Li. Clarkson was helpless as his mind projected back through time, reliving the moments when the two were close beyond discretion.

"I was going to bring some oblong tea." Mai Li uttered, nervous as a schoolgirl on her first date.

"I think that is the wrong punctuation."

"I know my newest friend pronounces it that way, and I like it. She also introduced me to this." And Mai Li had up a bottle of Pettibone Brandy.

"Then, by all means, come in. That same friend of yours says I need closure on the sudden realization that I had a son and the sudden loss coming so close together."

"Then, by all means, let's talk." Mai Li entered the room and closed the door.

Don't miss out!

Visit the website below and you can sign up to receive emails whenever Alex Mitchell publishes a new book. There's no charge and no obligation.

https://books2read.com/r/B-A-UGUAB-YHWXC

BOOKS 2 READ

Connecting independent readers to independent writers.

Also by Alex Mitchell

Welcome to Shepherds Pass
Revenge at Shepherds Pass
Treasure at Shepherds Pass
Welcome to Shepherds Pass
Man Among the Missing
Noreen Tyler
Robinhood at Shepherds Pass
That Which Makes Us Who We Are
Secrets That Bind Family
Balance of Power in Shepherds Pass
All Gods Children
The Mole Hunters Children
Anita Tyler and the Puzzles of Mass Destruction